ALSO BY MICHAEL E. PETRIE

*You're The Only One I Can Trust*

A BEN HARDING MYSTERY  BOOK TWO

# This Guy's the Limit

*A Novel*

## MICHAEL E. PETRIE

THIS GUY'S THE LIMIT
Copyright © 2024 Michael E. Petrie



Published by Dorus Mor Books

ISBN: 978-1-647048-46-4 (paperback)
ISBN: 978-1-647048-47-1 (hardcover)
ISBN: 978-1-647048-45-7 (eBook)

To L and the Kids

In remembrance of my late friend
and dynamic criminal defense attorney

The lawyer's a man of sorrow, and acquainted with grief;
Among all the sinners, he's considered the chief.
His friends all admire him when he conquers for them;
When he chances to lose, they're quick to condemn.
They say, "Ah! He is bought!" if he loses a case;
They say, "Ah! He is crooked!" if he wins in the race.
If he charges big fees, they say he's a grafter;
If he charges small fees, "He's not worth going after."
If he joins the church, "It's for an effect;"
If he doesn't join, "He's as wicked as heck."
But here is one fact we all must admit:
When we get into trouble, our lawyer is IT.

John W. Davis (1873–1955)

Connie Cantu-Gambil never had any trouble controlling men. And her husband was no exception. The three-carat diamond on the ring finger of her left-hand glittering in the sunlight could attest to that. No, the problem was not in how to control him; but rather, how to kill him. Had he been a sickly or elderly man, Connie might just have waited out the years for him to pass of natural causes. Patience was a virtue of her Hawaiian/Chinese/Filipino lineage. Unfortunately, her hapless spouse was young, vigorous, and healthy. So, the process was in need of speeding up. Connie needed to intervene.

She pondered this whilst lounging listlessly under a warm Hawaiian sun, reclined fetchingly atop a wicker chaise on board the luxury yacht owned by her soon-to-be late husband, Gavin Gambil. Their three-year marriage had run its course. Connie was ready to move on but intended to do so as a wealthy widow, the only living heir to her husband's fortune. *Only living heir* had a nice sound to it. The only reason her silly husband was wealthy at all was because of her, at least indirectly. He inherited his wealth upon the death of his older brother, a savvy businessman who had amassed a fortune through real estate dealings in Hawaii and California. It was the older brother, Griffin Gambil, with whom she'd first had a relationship. She smiled, reflecting back on her time with the now deceased brother: a middle-aged married man who was estranged from his wife, and obsessed with Connie. Obsessed with her island exoticness, her commanding demeanor, her Asianness. In time, Connie wagered back then, she would be able to gain access to much of his fortune. But then he went and died, leaving her in the lurch.

She had never felt any attraction to the younger brother, but Gavin was named in Griffin's will to inherit a large portion of his older brother's fortune and she decided to follow the money. Gavin was a deeply religious man. Bearing the burden and grief of losing his only brother was a true test of his faith. She capitalized upon what she viewed as his vulnerability, comforting him with acts of kindness and sharing verses from a Bible in which she had no belief, carefully calculated at guiding him into falling in love with her. They got married on the sands of Waikiki Beach like tourists, and Gavin used a portion of the substantial inheritance from his brother to purchase the yacht that was now their home. They named it the *Waay Mo' Bettah* when Connie moved from of her rented condo overlooking a golf course to take up residence aboard. Way more better indeed! Just follow the money. Griffin was dead, but the money remained. Sharing it with a spouse had been okay as a newlywed, but now it was time to claim it all for herself. One brother down, one to go.

Connie Cantu-Gambil never imagined she would ever marry a haole – a Hawaiian word meaning foreigner, but generally applied to Caucasians – and such a religious man to boot. The latter being the thing Connie found most annoying, and something she had real trouble tolerating on a daily basis. The smug nonstop sententious beatitudes: *Blessed are the pure of heart; Blessed are the meek; Blessed are the blah, blah, blah.* Worst of all, his sacrosanct born-again concern that prevented him from even enjoying his new-found wealth as much as she did: *it is easier for a camel to pass through the eye of a needle than for a rich man to enter the kingdom of God.* The man actually worried that he had too much wealth, often citing the Book of Job that nothing, not wealth, not health, *nothing* can remain forever. The only lesson Connie gleaned from that spiritual rhetoric was that, since nothing lasts forever, she must grab for all she can, in any way she can. She did not believe in Gavin's Christianity, nor the Buddhism in which she was raised, nor even the Hawaiian deity hierarchy that was everywhere in these islands. Jesus was no more believable than Pele, the volcano goddess whose eruptions mythically created all of Hawaii. Connie believed only in herself. And what Connie knew that Gavin did not was that she had skillfully choreographed his fall from grace without his even being aware. Gavin had unwittingly sold his soul to the devil and Connie had brokered the deal.

And now, as he did most mornings, Gavin was leaving to go fishing. Connie watched as he started the twin engines of his fishing skiff, the yacht's tender, christened *Bite Me* – a name Connie herself had chosen – and pulled away from the slip. He waved a cheerful farewell to Connie. She smiled falsely back, with exaggerated effort lifting her arm, responding perfunctorily, moving her hand in an emotionless royal wave. Gavin threw a kiss her way. Slowly shaking her head with lassitude at this pathetic gesture of affection, her smile glued in place until he was out of sight, then her waving stopped, her arm flopped down onto the chaise: dead weight.

Motoring out of Ala Wai Harbor under a cloudless blue sky, passing swaying palm trees lining the shore, Gavin was filled with anticipation of doing sporting battle against pelagic titans out on the deep blue ocean. Gavin most assuredly believed he was finally living the good life. He just had no idea ... no idea at all.

CHAPTER TWO

# BEN HARDING

Samantha Zimmer stood in the waning daylight, on the front deck of my California beachfront home, staring out toward endless ocean as the sun disappeared beyond the horizon and the sky began to take on a brilliant orange hue. Though I have observed this nightly spectacle of nature countless times before and never tire of it, I wanted Samantha to enjoy it in solitary appreciation, as if the encroaching dusk were her very own. So, I remained inside the house looking out at her there on the deck, breeze blowing her hair, gently ruffling her skirt. That's the image that springs into my mind every time I've thought about beautiful Samantha these past couple of years.

My fascination with Samantha Zimmer, though, goes all the way back to high school. She was, in my opinion, the most beautiful girl in our entire school. She was a couple of years younger, a mere freshman when I was a junior, but she captured my heart so completely that I traveled in her wake like a faithful puppy the rest of high school. Always paying just enough notice of me to keep my hopes up, but never quite following through with the sort of attention I craved from her, I prayed night after night to any deity who might listen that if I could just have one thing in this life – please God let me have Samantha Zimmer! Unfortunately, after graduation, it would be three decades before our paths would converge again. But I'm getting ahead of myself.

I guess it *really* all began about five years ago. That was when I inherited this old beach house from Uncle Jack, my favorite uncle. And that is when the life of yours truly, Ben Harding, made a serious course correction.

Uncle Jack was, I suppose, the miscreant black sheep of the family. Standing out amongst all my uptight, conservative, hard-working, ambitious, God-fearing relatives, Uncle Jack shone brightly like some blighted beacon of bohemian unconventionality. The family dismissed him as a crackpot, but I always admired him. Already well over thirty when the whole *hippie thing* was going on back in the late 1960s and early 70s, Uncle Jack embraced that youth subculture anyway – in spite of the "don't trust anyone over thirty" Zeitgeist dogma – shunning the mainstream, growing long hair and beard and "going with the flow" of the counterrevolutionaries. Long after the days of dope-smoking gurus and independent free spirits with long flowing locks had been replaced by, to borrow his expressions, *money-grubbing yuppies and capitalistic Gen-X'ers*, Uncle Jack retained the facial hair and the 60s attitude … and continued to live along a little strip of Venice Beach, California called Ocean Front Walk.

Many summers of my youth were spent at the funky little beach shack. As a kid, Uncle Jack taught me to surf the small but consistent wave breaks right in front of his house. By then Uncle Jack would have been in his late forties, or maybe even fifty, but you would never know it. He could surf with the best of them and bike ride along the beach bike path for hours.

And we would sit out on the front deck, day after sunshiny day, listening to rock music and flirting with bikini-clad beach bunnies as they cruised past our door on roller skates along the paved pathway that parallels the ocean for some twenty miles, before the sun finally sizzled into the Pacific right in front of us. Back then, everything and everybody at the beach just seemed so damned exciting!

The years passed. I went off to college, law school, got married, and started my legal career. Too many hours spent slaving away for an unappreciative law firm caused the marriage to spiral, crash and burn – terminating in divorce. In the blink of an eye, a quarter century had come and gone. I'd had little communication with Uncle Jack in all that time. When news reached me of his passing, I was deeply saddened. My knees caved, suddenly lacking ability to support my frame, tears rolling down my cheeks. Shortly afterwards, I discovered Uncle Jack had left a will.

I never imagined Uncle Jack would leave anything to me. Indeed, I never considered my freewheeling uncle to have accrued much of an estate. But there was the old beach house on Ocean Front Walk in Venice. What fun times we had shared there. And now the funky old house from my youth was mine – paid for, title free and clear.

There I was, well into my own forties, senior counsel in a law firm after decades of legal drone work, recently divorced, and living alone. Time for a major course correction and the beach house was my ticket. So, I quit my attorney job with a prestigious-but-boring California law firm, moved into Uncle Jack's beach house, and decided to become a part-time solo practitioner/full-time beach bum. Perhaps it was my way of paying homage to my late uncle, who knows? It was all working out pretty well until I became reunited, at age forty-eight, with the girl I'd coveted so much in high school, my first real love and the one I'd never quite gotten over: Samantha Zimmer.

I remember it vividly. I had just returned from a morning run along the beach and was scrolling through emails on my computer. Amongst the junk was a message that caught my eye. I'd been contacted about a thirty-year school reunion being planned. Thirty years! I was stunned that so much time had passed, and lamented how many of those years I had wasted in pursuit of the almighty dollar while life was passing me by. I felt as if I'd only recently been reborn, enjoying the sort of bohemian lifestyle that I imagined most of my corporate-climbing, married, children-raising peers would likely not understand. What on earth would I have in common with that crowd? I responded to the email that I would not been attending. *Too busy*, I lied. My reply led to a dozen or more messages from former classmates attempting to reconnect and urging me to attend. And then I spotted one on my screen that caused an involuntary ripple up my spine, like what the French call *frisson*. The subject header read: *from Samantha*. Just reading her name on the screen, even after so many years had passed, still caused my heart to race. That message, as well as all subsequent ones, from her are still in my email history. She wrote:

> *Dear Benjamin,*
>
> *I saw your name on the reunion list. My God, I can't believe how lucky it was to find you. So much has happened. I really need to see you. Even if you are not planning to attend your reunion, can we please meet?*
>
> *Samantha*

Yes, it was *my* thirty-year reunion. Hers was still a couple years away, but she apparently followed all the alumni announcements. I think I must have read her message at least five times, as if my brain was suffering from some sort of neuron disconnect and finding myself wondering whether a cosmic settlement was taking place: I was finally living the kind of carefree beach life I had always secretly dreamed of, and perhaps now the girl of my dreams would be entering this new utopia to share with me. But the voice of reason inside my head reminded me not to go reading too much into it, so I coolly replied: *Sure.* And we arranged to meet.

Much to my disappointment, it turned out that Samantha had not sought me out as an old boyfriend. Not as the love of her life who had gotten away. What she saw in me was someone who could assist with a legal situation she was embroiled in. A lawyer who would take a personal interest in her and her situation. She was hoping I might be that same hopelessly smitten teenaged boy she had known, only with a law degree.

Her well-to-do husband had passed away and she hired me to handle the probate of his estate. Probate was not really my area of legal expertise, though I'd handled a few in my career. There was still a fair amount of that smitten teenage boy left in me, and she had the kind of demeanor that made me want to help her, so I agreed.

It was the first time we had seen each other in all those years, and I think the realization that she was my one true love hit me the moment I set eyes on her again. Unfortunately, the circumstances of our reunion – that of putting in order the affairs of her recently deceased husband who, as it turned out, had not only been the victim of a murder but had left behind a rather complex inheritance situation – were not exactly conducive to romance, so I did not really push the agenda of re-sparking old feelings. I merely did my best to help her through a trying time as a good friend would, and to expedite the probate of the estate as a good lawyer should.

The inheritance complexity involved a handwritten will the husband had left behind. In that holographic will he left his entire estate to a woman he had apparently been seeing outside of his marriage: a mistress. Of course, legally he cannot leave community property to someone other than his wife. Even leaving non-community property to someone not a family member causes complexity. The mistress tried, under the handwritten will, to claim the remainder of the estate, the non-community portion, which was still a sizeable chunk of change. It took over a year to sort it all out. Samantha inherited her community portion, the mistress went away with nothing, and the remainder was inherited by the deceased's only sibling, a brother, according to a prior formally attested will that was ultimately upheld by the court. Throughout that year Samantha and I spent countless hours together and, full disclosure, I enjoyed each and every minute.

Unfortunately, after the probate was settled and she had no further need of my legal services, I seemed to fall off her radar screen. I took it as a sign that she was not interested in me in any romantic sense. I accepted that as fact and made myself scarce. Another year went by. It was then that another course correction occurred in my life: I turned fifty.

The day before my birthday, the last day I would spend as a forty-something man before plunging across the half-century mark, was exceptionally warm and sunny for late October. I was shirtless and barefoot, wearing only baggy board shorts, giving my car – a Porsche Cabriolet, ocean blue – a much needed bath in the alley behind my house which parallels the sandy beach that is my front yard. I was bent over, scrubbing the rear spoiler, when a VW Jetta convertible pulled up alongside and stopped with its front wheel directly atop the hose I was using, immediately cutting off the water supply.

"Hey!" I grumbled, looking up annoyed but quickly noticing the errant driver had a strikingly pretty face and long honey colored hair. She looked to be around twenty-five ... *half my age*, my brain quickly computed.

"Sorry," she said smiling, rolling her car forward a few inches, water once again flowing from the hose. She remained behind the wheel, still smiling, and looking my way.

"Can I help you?" I asked with avuncular intonation.

"I hope so. I'm a little lost. I'm on my way to a party, it's at this address on Speedway Street," she answered pleasantly, holding up a crumpled piece of paper with writing too small for me to read from four feet away.

Turning off the hose, I walked over to her car. Leaning in to read the address on the paper she held flattened against her steering wheel, my eyes also caught sight of shapely thighs and a very short skirt. "That address is just a bit farther down the beach, not far. You're almost there," I said, pointing northward up the alley.

I stopped leaning and straightened up to go back and resume my car washing task. She continued to sit in her car, staring blankly at the address paper pressed to her steering wheel.

"Really," I added, "it's only a few blocks. Just continue down this alley until you come to 30th Street and hang a left."

A few more seconds of staring at the paper, then she turned and flashed an incredible smile my way. "I don't really know anybody at this party. And you seem nice. Wanna come with me?"

Now, I've never really fancied myself as much of a ladies' man, truly, so this stopped me dead in my tracks. Several seconds went by, perhaps with my mouth agape, wondering if she was just having some fun with me. As I came to grips with the notion that the invitation was genuine, my brain flashed *half my age* again, this time more as a warning than a mere calculation.

"How do you know I'm nice?" I asked. "You don't even know my name."

"I'm usually a pretty good judge of people. It's a talent I have. Trust me, you're nice. So, tell me then. What *is* your name?"

"Ben," I answered. "Ben Harding."

"Is that like James ... James Bond?" She giggled. "I'm Heather. Heather Thomas."

Want to know the best birthday present in the world to give a man about to hit fifty? Try a flirtatious invitation to a party by a beautiful woman half his age. "Okay," I muttered stupidly. "Party beats car washing any day."

I rolled up the hose and drove my partially washed car back into the garage. I knew finding a place to park on the crowded streets along the beach on such a beautiful day as this would be nearly impossible, so suggested she park in my garage as well. "You can park right next to me."

"Right next to you. I like the way that sounds," she purred jokingly.

"It'll probably be easier to walk to this shindig than to drive the few blocks anyway."

"Shindig? That's funny." She had a cute laugh.

We went inside the house so I could throw on a shirt and change into shorts that were not speckled with car grease and water spots, but we never made it to the party. She pulled a joint from her purse, I poured us some wine, and we quickly found our way to the bedroom. And that is where we stayed for the next dozen or so hours.

As the new morning sun rose, rays through the window

showered her with heavenly light, illuminating the youthful perfection of a body firm and unblemished, but for the tattoo splashed across her backside. I watched her lying next to me, breathing. Her breasts rising and falling. I had not been with anyone like her, nor experienced anything like this since … well, perhaps never. To say it was amazing would be a gross under evaluation, at least from my perspective. Best birthday gift? You guessed it.

I had gotten out of bed and was just returning from my morning stand-up routine in the loo. Sitting up in bed, a sheet pulled up to her chin, she was watching me walk back across the room.

"Good morning," I said.

"You've got a great body," she responded, matter-of-factly. "But I guess you must already know that, huh. You work out?"

Want to know another best birthday gift? To have a gorgeous girl half your age in bed naked, and she tells you how great *your* body is.

"Uh, thanks. I run, I surf, ride my bike. You know, standard beach life stuff. In case you weren't aware of it, I noticed your body before you even got out of the car yesterday."

"I was sorta counting on that," she giggled.

"This has gotta be the best birthday ever," I gushed, when she snuggled next to me as I crawled back into bed.

"Birthday?" she asked.

"Today is officially my birthday," I answered.

"How old? No, no. Let me guess. Forty?" She asked.

I blushed.

"No, no. It's okay. I kinda like older men. It's okay if you're forty. I don't mind."

"I think I love you, but you're a decade off. Today I turn the big five-oh."

"Fifty?" she asked.

"Fifty," I confirmed.

"Fifty," she repeated, incredulity saturating the word.

"Fifty," I sighed, incredulity attaching to my rendition as well.

"Wow, you're the oldest guy I've ever had sex with." I noticed she didn't say "made love with." From her perspective this was just sex and she had now set the record for being with the oldest dude ever. For me it was a trip to heaven, bolstering my libido to that of a damn teenager, an absolutely perfect way to usher in being fifty!

"Jesus, fifty," I heard her mutter to herself, as if she'd just committed a crime – whatever is the opposite of child statutory rape.

"I'm flattered you think I look so much younger," I said, planting a kiss on her forehead.

Turning her face toward me, studying mine a moment, she replied, "No, I guess you look around fifty. It's just, the Porsche, living at the beach, your dark tan ... you know, you have a youthful ... what's the right word? Facade. You have a youthful facade. You look great ... for somebody your age, I mean. Great shape, too, for a man of ...," she hesitated a fraction of a moment, "fifty."

That's when it hit me. It's all a facade. I may not feel fifty. I may not act fifty. Perhaps I don't even look fifty ... but I most certainly *am* fifty. Want to truly know the best gift you can give a man on his fiftieth birthday? A reality check.

I suddenly knew, right there and then, that my life was in need of yet another course correction. I decided my foray into the beach good-life needed some adjustment. I had no business being bed partners with a *girl* young enough to be my daughter. My life should have more complexity than merely wondering whether the surf was up, like some teenage wave rider. Or driving a two-seater sports car, like some sad middle-aged moron flexing automotive muscle. My life needed more substance. A lot more.

Also, at fifty I finally realized that *time's a wastin'* regarding other goals and aspirations. Things that had been shelved for some later date. If there ever was a right time to declare my intentions and affections for the love of my life – Samantha Zimmer – it was now!

Next thing I knew, we were both out of bed, getting dressed. A final kiss on the cheek from her and she was out the door, backing her car from my garage, a girlish wave of her hand as she drove away. "Bye-Bye Ben Harding. Happy birthday!"

## CHAPTER THREE

# BEN HARDING

No sooner had Heather and I bid *adieu* than I was dialing Samantha on my cell phone. Crap! Voice mail. I remained silently on the line for a long moment, not sure whether to leave a message, before pressing the little red button on my phone to end the call.

Walking alone along the sand in the direction of Marina del Rey, passing the Venice Pier, trying to conjure up some sort of cohesive plan for wooing Samantha, I found myself in front of a Polynesian-themed condo complex with lots of tropical foliage and bubbling waterfalls. This is where my friend Vincent G. Scatucci lives. Handsome and smart, Vinnie and I met a couple years or so ago at a party in the marina. The kind of guy who is so disarmingly charismatic he makes you feel like you are life-long buddies right from the get-go. Instantly engaging, his voice and manner pleasant, yet his language racy and incisive, but with a sort of comic relief giving a certain feeling of unreality to any conversation. He seemed to me like a young Al Pacino when we had first met, and I told him so. He laughed, waved his arms around like he was embracing the entire room and emoted, "Why does everybody tell me that? I guess I just gotta live with it." Discovering we had a lot of things in common – both lawyers, both around the same age – and just enough differences between us to keep it interesting – Vincent, a sharp-dressed criminal defense attorney who loves his job; while I mostly wear shorts, flip-flops, and have all but given up practicing law – we became fast friends.

I wandered a few steps into the complex. Style-wise it was resort meets bordello, complete with scantily clad ladies draped about the pool area. I spotted Scatucci seated amongst a banquet of faux-wicker deck chairs. He was busily conversing with a top-heavy brunette in a thong bikini. Spotting me, he waived me over, greeting me, as is his usual custom, with a manly embrace of exaggerated welcoming, "Ah, *paesano!*"

If turning fifty while in the company of a girl half my age was an epiphany that I should grow up and settle down before it's too late, my friend Vincent Scatucci must have somehow experienced, somewhere along the way, the exact opposite epiphany: The guy is almost always in the company of beautiful women, many of whom are barely drinking age. "Being a lawyer is like catnip to women," he once told me. "Best thing I ever did was become a lawyer!" Aphoristic, perhaps, but I knew it had not always been thus. Told to me in choppy installments over many pitchers of beer, over a period of several months, I'd learned quite a bit about my friend's long and winding road toward his métier.

In a nutshell: Growing up in Michigan, dropping out of college to marry his pregnant girlfriend, and becoming a Detroit policeman. "Detroit was a fucking cesspool," he told me with a thick Detroit accent. "Still is. Not enough cops in the whole world to make it a safe place to live. Couldn't wait to get outa there." Then a job with the FBI that included a stint as an undercover agent for the Drug Enforcement Agency and a lot of time spent in faraway cities. "The war on drugs? It was ridiculous. I was doing more drugs than the guys I was sent to bust. But it was not a fun time." Being away from home for long periods took a toll on his marriage. "Came home one time and found my wife with another guy. I threw him out a second story window. Put him in the fuckin' hospital. I kinda felt pretty bad about that. I mean, it wasn't that asshole's fault. A stiff dick has no conscience, know what I mean? He was just doin' what any guy would do if given the opportunity. It was my cheating wife who I should'a chucked through that window." Then divorce. "She claimed I was an unfit father in a dangerous profession and should not have any custody of my daughter. Courts always side with the mutha, ya know? A woman's gotta be one sorry piece of shit to lose custody of her kid. A man just has to have a dangerous job and a bit of a temper." His daughter, Gina, was the person he loved most in the entire world. "I love my parents; I love my older sister; there was a time when I loved my wife. But when Gina was born ... wow! That's when I felt the kind of love I never knew existed before. You don't have kids, Ben. So, you can't possibly know. Ya gotta become a parent to know the kind of intense feeling I'm talkin' about here."

He needed a less dangerous career if he wanted any sort of custody of his daughter. So, Scatucci returned to school at night, finishing his college degree, then on to law school, also part-time at night, focusing on criminal law. "Law school was really hard, but it still beat being a cop. Nobody was gonna to shoot me if I failed an exam." I told him that Stanford was my alma mater. He just shook his head, as if feeling sorry for me. "Listen *paesan*, I may have graduated bottom of my night school class from probably the worst law school in California," he said laughing, "but in a courtroom I'm not intimidated in the least by those guys in their conservative pin-striped suits and repp ties who went to Stanford or Yale or any of those snotty schools. Know why? Because I have something they don't: The inside scoop on cops, because I used to be one of 'em. I know exactly how cops think and know just how to use that against them in a criminal proceeding. Something you just can't learn at law school."

That knowledge apparently serves Scatucci very well in his practice. His big break came about ten years ago, representing an independent automobile manufacturer who was developing and marketing a brand-new type of sport car. "Only came in one color and had gull-wing doors that flipped up when nobody else did that," he explained. "Great looking vehicle. But the car was slow to catch on and the guy's company was bleeding money. So, he sold drugs on the side in order to raise cash to support his fledgling company. The guy got busted for selling to some undercover cops." It was a somewhat high-profile case, covered on the local TV news. Scatucci got him acquitted, proving entrapment by the police. "It just smelled of entrapment. The hard part was proving it. Judges don't like to rule against police, but I was able to show them the light."

With the notoriety of that case, a steady flow of clients followed. Scatucci now has all the outward trappings of a big-time criminal defense lawyer: his own firm located in a plush office building on Wilshire Boulevard in Beverly Hills, not to mention the condo at the beach with two expensive cars in the garage – a stately black BMW 750 il and a rocket-red Ferrari, á la Magnum P.I. No wonder he loves being a lawyer so much. But he keeps his business lean, employing only a single law clerk/paralegal and one receptionist/secretary. It's been a revolving door series of receptionists/secretaries, with most seeming to last not more than a few months.

However, Randy Rivlen, the law clerk, has been with Scatucci for over a decade. Rivlen was actually a formerly convicted felon who had a serious gambling addiction, sold drugs to support his habit, and had spent time in prison for embezzlement. Not long after his release, he was arrested yet again. Some guys never learn, it seems. This time Scatucci represented him, and he walked. Somehow the two became friends and Scatucci trained him in the law. "The guy is actually brilliant when it comes to researching and writing. He'd make a great lawyer, but his felony conviction puts the total kibosh on that. And since no other law firm is gonna hire a felon, he's stuck working for me. Which makes me lucky, cuz he does all the grunt work and I get to have all the courtroom fun."

As for his daughter, who was the reason Scatucci became a lawyer in the first place, she's now in her early twenties and they still spend every other weekend together. Otherwise, she lives with her mother somewhere over in San Bernadino County. I've only met her a few times, but she seems like a good kid.

I sat myself down into one of the deck chairs as the brunette in the thong stood up. Tall with seemingly infinite legs, she made a mild production out of wrapping a towel around her waist and left. "I'll give you a call mid-week," Scatucci called after her. She replied with a departing two-fingered peace wave over her shoulder as she disappeared back onto the beach.

"New squeeze?" I asked.

"Naw. She's a client. Ever heard of Bambini Bella?"

"The madam to the stars? Sure. I saw the story on the news about her. That she'd been arrested for running a high-priced call girl operation. You're her lawyer?"

Taking a hit from a beer bottle, smiling smugly, "Sure enough, paesano. Bambini Bella is a sobriquet. Her real name is Claire Annette Michaelson."

"Claranet, sounds like a wind instrument," I interrupt.

"I know, right?" he agrees, starting to laugh. "Claranet! Ha! A clarinet … that's a long hard instrument you put in your mouth and blow!" In this more enlightened age, Scatucci remains firmly rooted at inappropriate cave man humor. Laughing now so hard it evolves into coughing. Catching his breath, "Ah, well, maybe that's why she prefers to go by Bambini Bella. Anyway, I represented her a few years ago on another charge. More or less a garden variety pimping case that also involved attempted theft and some bounced checks. No real biggie. Got her off, so to speak." A momentary pause accompanied by a sly smile to be sure I caught the double entendre. "So, of course she came back. Another satisfied customer."

"Hmm, interesting clientele," I remarked, dryly.

"Hey, drug dealers and madams, it's what pays the bills my friend."

I smiled with a deprecatory nod.

"What?" he responded, innocently. "Hey, I'm the good guy here. I'm the fucking knight in shining armor, the one making sure those accused of wrongdoing get all the due process they are entitled to under that grandest of documents, the United States Constitution."

I nodded again, this time concurring. "Probably a lot more interesting than all the bullshit corporate law I used to do."

"Ha! Of that, *paesan*, I have no doubt. Somebody once said that there are over a million novels that have been written, yet there are only seven basic plots. Can you believe it? Only seven. I can assure you that if the door of this lawyer's closet was ever opened, the world's stock of tragedies and comedies would be enormously increased."

Another nod from me. I tend to do a lot of nodding when I'm around Vinnie.

We sat around the pool shooting the shit, drinking beers. I

didn't mention that it was my birthday but did tell him about the girl I'd been with all night and morning. He gave me a wink of male approval and didn't seem surprised, as we clinked beer bottles. It was probably a perfectly normal everyday experience for him. I also never mentioned my epiphany, or that I could not get Sammie out of my mind. It had been a couple hours, I needed to try calling her again, so made my exit.

"Gotta go, bro. Good luck with the Bambini case. Thanks for the beer."

"*Ciao* buddy," he answered. "Keep it real."

Walking the beach, dialing Sammie. "Hello?" I heard her say.

CHAPTER FOUR

Connie Cantu-Gambil had lived all her life in Hawaii. Except for a brief time spent in Southern California, living at a place called Encino – a Spanish word meaning oak tree. An appropriately named place, she remembered thinking at the time, since she had moved there at the request of a man who was big and powerful like an oak: Griffin Gambil, her current husband's older brother. Griffin was tall, attractive, arrogant, and wealthy. He had but one major weakness: a concupiscent need for submitting to sexually dominant women, an S&M fetish commonly referred to as Female Domination. Since his wife of nearly fifteen years had no interest in indulging this fetish, he often sought satisfaction elsewhere. And so it was that Griffin and Connie met when Griffin was in Honolulu on a business trip and finding himself in need of satisfying his paraphilia. Mistress Cantu, as she was known in the S&M community back then, was in the business of granting male wishes for subordination at the rate of two hundred dollars an hour. She was a professional dominatrix with a reliable stable of obsequious clients: her sex slaves.

She recalled that first meeting as if it were yesterday. Griffin had originally contacted her on the internet. She used to have a web site where she acted as cyber-mistress, an internet dominatrix. She invited men to contact her through e-mail. Typically, she and they would send little S&M-flavored erotic messages back and forth, her generally referring to the guy as her slave and order him to do certain tasks. Once she had a guy hooked, she would demand some sort of tribute, a gift perhaps, but more often a monetary tribute. She maintained a mail drop where the slaves could send the tribute. On rare occasions, after developing rapport with a slave over an extended period and feeling comfortable that he was not some sort of dangerous psycho, she might agree to an in-person meeting. The slave would be required to fill out an application for such a session. She always made it clear there would be no sexual contact, but men were willing to pay money just to meet with her and to subjugate themselves to her.

That's how she initially met Griffin. On the internet he submitted an application for an in-person session. He said he would be traveling to Hawaii on business and asked to meet.

They met at a hotel on Kuhio Street in Waikiki where she often arranged for such sessions in those days. The manager was a brutish man who she was able to charm into being her defender, to handle any slave clients who might turn nasty, should the need arise.

The first time she saw Griffin she was somewhat surprised. He was handsome for a man of his years and quite tall, over six feet. He was dressed in a dark business suit, unusual for mainland visitors to Hawaii who generally showed up in shorts and bright-colored aloha shirts. And he exhibited a no-nonsense, gruff, almost angry demeanor. A real tough-guy type. His physical presence did not fit with the docile persona of the slave she had come to know through e-mail correspondence. Griffin swaggered into the hotel lobby like some macho John

Wayne character ... until he saw her. Their eyes met and he immediately knew who she was. She did not need to be in some stereotypical leather fetish outfit, just seeing her stopped him dead in his tracks, instantly transforming to docility.

He followed her meekly to her hotel room. Once inside, she ordered him to remove all his clothing and assume a kneeling position. He did so without hesitation. For the next hour she subjected her slave to intense verbal humiliation and emasculating behavior. Through it all he remained fully aroused. Griffin wasn't into torture or flogging or any of the other pain avenues associated with S&M. He just liked to be ordered around by a strong, dominant woman.

As that first hour was nearing its end, she assumed her slave needed sexual release. So, she ordered him to begin masturbating, on his knees, at her feet. He was forbidden from climaxing without her permission, however. If he disobeyed, she threatened they would never see one another again. Before long he was pleading for permission to cum. His eyes rolled upward in his head and his body appeared to be convulsing, even as his hand continued pumping up and down like a piston. "Please mistress," he pathetically implored. "I am begging for your permission."

She asked her groveling slave what he would do to earn permission for release. She already knew the answer. He would have agreed to do anything to get her permission. Of course, he did not really *need* her permission. This was just a part of the game. She asked how much money he had in his wallet. "A thousand dollars," he answered, adding that she could have it all if she would simply grant permission for him to climax. True to his promise, he handed her ten one-hundred-dollar bills. No slave had ever paid that much for a single hour of her time. She knew right then that Griffin was a man of means. She had discovered a gold mine.

Griffin could easily afford a great deal of her time and, with frequent trips to the island paradise, quickly became a regular client. His fetish toward female domination was like a drug to him. The more humiliating the task she demanded, the greater the high he seemed to derive from it. Each successive session became more intense than the last. To show his appreciation he gave her jewelry and clothing in addition to cash. After one particularly intense session that lasted all weekend, he handed her the keys to a new Mercedes Benz with her name on the title.

A year passed, Griffin's Hawaii business dealings were concluding. He began coaxing her to leave Hawaii and move to the mainland – to California – so they could continue being together. He offered to buy her a house where she could live and they could continue their sessions in absolute privacy, away from hotel rooms. The offer included ample spending money in exchange for the exclusivity of her services. Without hesitation, she accepted. She had found her golden goose and was not inclined to let him slip away.

On the mainland, they then spent so much time together that Griffin's wife left him because he was almost never home. It was a legal separation that seemed headed toward divorce. He was happy for the wife to be gone, more time to spend with his dominant mistress. As long as Griffin remained alive and obsessed with her, Connie Cantu was living on Easy Street.

Then, one afternoon, she walked out onto the front lawn of the house he had gifted her and saw him lying in a pool of blood near his car parked in the street at the end of her driveway. He had driven over to see her but never made it to the front door. Murdered, much of his head blown off. An apparent drive-by shooting in the normally low-crime Encino neighborhood. She could tell immediately that he was dead, and Connie felt her world instantly collapsing around her. What would happen now? But the police soon thereafter discovered a handwritten will in the glovebox of Griffin's car bequeathing his entire fortune to *her*. All that money now hers!

Connie's heart was beating so hard with excitement at this turn of events she feared it might pop right out of her chest. Her expectations were quickly challenged, however, by Griffin's wife, who was livid to discover not only her husband's affair – so *this* is why he was never home! – but that he attempted to leave his entire estate to this stranger. Lawyers got involved. The wife also accused Connie of murdering her husband to get the inheritance. The protracted legal battle eventually ended with Connie inheriting nothing. The police never seriously considered Connie a murder suspect, but even after the actual murderer was eventually apprehended and convicted, the wife continued to hold firm to her belief that Connie was somehow involved.

It was shortly after all those horrific events that Connie remembered meeting the younger brother, Gavin … and hope of reclaiming the Gambil fortune was renewed. The wife may have gotten half of Griffin's estate, but it was the brother who got the other half.

Gavin was the polar opposite of his older brother. Gavin was not tall, not particularly handsome, and certainly not clever at business. Though he had a wearing-his-heart-on-his-sleeve sort of niceness about him, he exhibited extreme disdain for Connie, seemingly blaming her for the death of his brother. He was well aware of the, in his judgment, *sordid* relationship his brother had with Connie and, being a devoutly Christian man, it pained Gavin that his brother had fallen under the spell of someone he considered to be a common whore, an instrument of the devil who had been leading Griffin down the path to hell! Gavin viciously chastised her for leading his brother astray, subjecting her to voracious tirades on the wages of sin, hurling Bible verses like lightning bolts. At first she thought this fellow was some sort of raving lunatic, spouting off all this religious mumbo jumbo at her. But this brother of Griffin kept hammering away at her. He made it his mission in life to reform her and bring her to Jesus. She decided to allow him to believe his efforts were working.

Gavin was pleased with what he perceived as Connie's receptive reaction to the teachings of the Lord. With the representation of Connie as a changed woman, Gavin believed he had shown Connie the road to salvation. He believed Connie Cantu, not unlike the Biblical Mary Magdalene whom Jesus saved from a life of sinful debauchery, experienced what appeared to be a powerful religious conversion. If pride had not been a sin, Gavin would certainly have felt proud for turning her around.

Since it was in her very nature to be controlling, she began maneuvering the situation to her advantage, leading him toward falling in love with her. Gavin married the newly converted Connie on the beach in Hawaii, where they might have lived happily ever after ... except that, unlike Mary Magdalene – who loved Jesus and followed Him through thick and thin, even as she watched Him toil under the burden of carrying a heavy cross through Jerusalem, watched Him die a miserable death upon that same cross, and was the first to discover His resurrection from the tomb – Connie's religious conversion was illusory. She quickly tired of Gavin and his garrulous religiosity, had no intention of hanging around through thick and thin, and began overtures toward reclaiming her old life.

With Gavin out fishing for the day, Connie sat alone on the yacht. Opening her laptop, there were more than a dozen emails from new slaves. She had only recently revived her online presence and already these twisted souls had discovered her. Males are such weird creatures, she thought to herself scanning the messages. Their entire universe seemed to be centered upon one small appendage located between their legs that has a direct uninterrupted connection to their brains. Connie catered to those males with a kink in that connection, a bit of faulty wiring if you will. She'd had clients who enjoyed nothing better than a swift kick to the balls, or who liked to be slapped around, spanked, mummified, diapered, and/or cross dressed. Some even requested to be urinated upon, something for which Connie charged extra. The common theme to all of it was something most normal men would likely hate: loss of power. Throw in some humiliation and you've got the perfect client for a professional dominatrix, such as her.

Connie often found herself shaking her head in amused bewilderment at the strange requests she received. Though, she had to admit, perhaps she had a bit of short circuit in her own wiring, because she truly did enjoy objectifying males, inflicting both mental and physical pain, testing their limits, reducing them to groveling slaves ... and to then get paid for it was most satisfying of all.

She typed an email reply to the slave she liked to call Sissy, because of his penchant for forced sissification. Sissy's particular fetish was for Mistress Cantu to force him to dress in female attire. At less than five feet tall, there is no earthly way Connie could physically *force* her much taller, stronger male slave to do anything. But the illusion of being forced is what Sissy was totally into — erotic psychological manipulation, what might clinically be called masochistic transvestitism. There was nothing at all effeminate about this slave, including his heavy dark five o'clock shadow, the tonsure of flesh atop his head, a hairy chest and mid-life pot belly. So, when dressed as a woman he looked utterly ridiculous. A cross-dressing lumberjack right out of Monty Python. But his goal was not to look like or become an actual female. It was the mental emasculation and erotic humiliation of being forced to wear feminine attire that got him off, feeling powerless and under the control of a dominatrix. To varying degrees, this is what all her clients craved: sexual domination.

In real life, however, Sissy was certainly no sissy. A cocksure swagger and references to owning several successful businesses, among them an involvement in the illegal drug trade, gave him an almost dangerous patina. His real name was Edward Emsch, or Eddy as he preferred to be called by others who knew him, though he never disclosed that identity to Connie, keeping such information to himself as a scintilla of privacy. He only identified himself to her as Sissy. But after many months of sessions with Mistress Cantu, of prancing around in a fluffy pink party dress and Mary Jane shoes, Eddy had developed such a sense of trust with his mistress as he felt with no one else on earth. He had allowed her to know a side of him that no one else could ever be allowed to know. He trusted her explicitly. So much so that, returning to his more manly persona immediately after removing the feminine accouterments and coming down from his forced-fem high, perhaps as some sort of counterbalance to the submissive slave side he had allowed her to witness, he would often share with his mistress certain details with bravado, indeed to the point of outright braggadocio, about his macho exploits involving drug dealers and criminal connections.

It was during one of these after-session chats, after Sissy was put away and Eddy reemerged, that Connie began to formulate a plan for the elimination of her husband by using her ability to manipulate this slave.

On her keyboard Connie typed: *Sissy, I will be able to meet with you today at 2:00. Usual place. I have something very special*

*I want you to do for me today. Be certain not to disappoint me.
Mistress Cantu.*

## CHAPTER FIVE

Eddy Emsch sat leaning against a fluffy white pillow, legs outstretched on the bed of his hotel suite high up in the Rainbow Tower at the Hilton Hawaiian Village overlooking Waikiki Beach. A truly magnificent view that included the wide sandy beach, the azure Pacific, and the adjacent yacht harbor. But he wasn't looking out at the view. His eyes were on the laptop computer screen balanced on his lap, reading an email that just arrived from Mistress Cantu. In his gut there was that unmistakable, unshakable feeling: that feeling of overwhelming need. He'd been experiencing it for decades, since adolescence in fact. The inexplicable need to relinquish all power to a member of the so-called weaker sex, to feel helpless, worthless, belittled in her presence. To be in her control. He would have thought that by age forty he might have outgrown the need, but it was as strong as ever. In fact, as a successful businessman with the wherewithal to feed his fantasy, the intensity of the need had grown ever greater. He both hated and immensely enjoyed the feeling. Though he had no idea what even caused such a need, he had learned long ago the only way to deal with it was to embrace and indulge.

He'd also learned to mask his fetish over the years by

assuming a sometimes gruff overtly macho persona toward women. Many were the youthful relationships that ended because he had crossed the line by being too brutish toward a girlfriend. As he matured, he learned just how close to that line he could get without completely alienating affection altogether. His relationship with his spouse was a strong one, he had finally mastered the art. But the secret compulsion toward his sexual submissiveness remained. Like a patient seeking psychological help from a trusted therapist, finding the right woman to fulfill this fantasy, one who could truly be trusted, was essential. His wife was not that woman. She looked up to him as a strong man, a provider, smart and clever. He could never risk diminishing himself to her. He was certain there was no way she would accept his kinky foible without thinking less of him as a husband.

To his great relief, he found this fantastic Asian woman right here in Hawaii who seemed to completely *get him*. She understood him better than anyone he had ever met, and he felt completely comfortable releasing his needs unto her. He'd discovered her purely by chance while on a Hawaiian vacation a few years ago. The need had emerged and, even though his wife was an attractive woman and a fine lover in a conventional sense, she was unable to satisfy him once his submissive feelings emerged.

It was on an internet web site that he found the Asian woman. A professional dominatrix. The need was strong and he thought to himself, why not? Nobody knew him on this island. It was less risky than back in California where he was known, where he had a greater chance of being discovered. So, he contacted Mistress Cantu. After lengthy email communications, she agreed to see him in person. He was initially startled by her appearance. She was a dwarf-like woman. So much so that he was initially put off by her diminutive stature. But with a hard demeanor of total confidence, professionalism, and impenetrable air of superiority, she quickly took over, completely tuning in to his needs and satisfying him in ways he'd hardly dared to imagine. She even removed any guilt he might feel about his perversion, telling him, early on, *Never be ashamed. Hamsters can fuck, it takes an intelligent human being to have perversions.*

Then, she suddenly vanished from the internet, went dark, radio silent. Every search tool he tried came up empty. There was no way to find her. He felt like a heroin addict cut off from a supplier. He tried sessions with other professional doms but was never able to obtain the same level of intensity he had with that particular Asian lady.

After a long absence, she suddenly reemerged. Finding her again on the internet, he contacted her immediately. Several trumped-up business trips to Hawaii followed so he could be with her. And now, just reading this current email from her filled him with excitement. In just a few hours he would be in sub-space, a term coined by Mistress Cantu that so accurately described the submissive place she always led him to, where he could shed all inhibitions and pretensions. An almost out of body experience where he could watch himself morph into something unrecognizable and give himself completely to his mistress. When he was in sub-space, Mistress Cantu completely owned him, and he would do whatever she commanded.

Typing his reply: *Thank You Mistress. I will not disappoint you. Humbly yours, Sissy.*

Eddy, of course, had no way of knowing that his mistress was receiving that reply while lounging on her yacht located in the harbor within easy view of his hotel window. He could have just as easily written his reply on a piece of hotel stationery, folded it into a paper airplane and flown it out the window and down to her. Also, he had no idea the magnitude of what her demands of him would be that day and what it would take not to disappoint her.

## CHAPTER SIX

They met at the usual place, a small studio apartment overlooking the Ala Wai Canal. Common minds in a depraved synchronization; one dominant and controlling, the other submissive and obedient. A euphoric two-hour session of sissified prancing, dainty mincing, twirling and curtseying, wearing a pink ruffled dress with a large bow tied in back and bouncy petticoat beneath that the mistress had purchased from a store catering to square dancers – the apogee leaving him completely spent, wiped out, exhausted.

The aftermath, as always, was a feeling of light-headedness, calmness, relaxation, and well-being. The way people often feel after an hour with their shrink, or doing yoga, or right after a really great massage – only more so. The transformation from Sissy back to Eddy always felt like emerging from a hazy dreamlike place and returning back to harsh reality. But this time Sissy had made a promise to Mistress Cantu that Eddy was expected to carry out. Coming down, returning to being Eddy, the gravitas of his promise slowly sinking in: *She wants me to kill someone.*

"I don't just go around killing people," he found himself telling her, Eddy's manly self completely back now. "Maybe

I could just rough him up a bit. Why do you want him dead anyway?"

"You no never mind. It's my business. You just do what you promised," she responded, slipping as she sometimes does, from the Queen's English to the pidgin dialect so common to Hawaii. "You no need worry. Nobody will miss him. Nobody will even notice him missing." She jotted some info onto a small white card and handed it to Emsch. "You go to dat slip numba at Ala Wai Marina tonight. You will find a small fishing boat tied up near a large yacht. Name on da back transom is *Bite Me*. Do something to mess up the engine on that smaller boat so that it will quit after running a couple hours or so."

"Do what? I'm no boat mechanic."

"Not my problem. I know nothing about boat engines, either. Just make it happen. Tonight. Must be tonight. Email me a message when you are done. I will give further instructions to you then." With that, she strode confidently out of the room, taking the square dance garments with her, leaving him sitting alone and naked, holding the paper card she had given him.

The sun had set, and Gavin was already back from his day of fishing, when Connie returned to the yacht. "How your day wen?" her pidgin greeting, accepting his kiss to her offered cheek.

"Good day for fishing, unfortunately not such a good day for catching," he replied with a grin, sipping a beer and shaking his head from side to side. He had only caught one smallish tuna. "But you know what they say, *the worst day fishing still beats the best day working*." He laughed out loud at his own quip.

She smiled at him. "Well," she chided, "if you are not man enough to bring home dinner, then I guess we will have to go out to eat. Besides, there is some shopping I wanna do. First, we'll shop, then have dinner at that new place in Kahala."

He hated shopping and did not care much for the fancy

eating joints in posh Kahala, but he adored her. Giving her cheek another peck, replied, "It's a date. Let me shower and change, then we'll go out on the town and have fun."

Walking out onto the aft deck of the floating home she shared with her husband, looking up at the tropical sky, she noticed there was no moon, though planets and stars shone overhead in the darkened celestial expanse with diamond brilliance. Connie loved diamonds, a girl's best friend for certain, she believed. "Take your time," she called after him as he headed for the shower, "we've got all evening." All evening, indeed, she thought to herself. No need to return till I get an email from my obedient slave that he has completed his task.

CHAPTER SEVEN

Early morning. Heading for open water at a leisurely cruising speed, Gavin was in his element: sunlight glistening off turquoise water, a sea speckled with white crests like the manes of ethereal white stallions, loaves of puffy clouds in the cerulean sky above. He imagined that this was what the glorious afterlife might be like, except he would be fishing with Jesus.

The fish-finder alarm on the boat suddenly went off. A school of mahi mahi – dolphin fish, dorado they are called on the mainland – was just under his skiff. He slowed down, killed the engines, and dropped his fishing lines over the side of the boat. Hooking up almost immediately, a brilliantly colored mahi of iridescent turquoise, yellow, and green was leaping out of the water, gyrating, splashing color across his line of vision reminiscent of a show he watched on TV as a boy: *Disney's Wonderful World of Color*. Gavin reeled the fish closer. The fish twisted, turned, and fought hard, but it was no match for the skilled angler.

Pulling on board fish after fish he found himself shouting into the wind, "Wow! Where were all these fish yesterday?" Yesterday he had returned home nearly empty-handed. Now, today, there were already six huge dolphin fish in the boat's cooler. Gavin figured this must just be his lucky day. Thank you, Lord!

At some point, they ceased biting, the fish-finder on the boat indicating no more fish in the immediate vicinity. Time to motor up and find a new spot to fish. Turning the key to restart the engines … nothing. Gavin had spared no expense in outfitting the fishing boat of his dreams. "The sky's the limit," he told the yacht dealer as he rattled off the impressive list of optional equipment to add to the standard features included in the vessel Gavin was purchasing. So, he was more than a bit disgruntled when, on this particular day that had so-far been his "lucky" day with hours of fantastic fishing, the boat now bobbed up and down, gyrating with the waves in a swirling motion.

Three hours outside of Honolulu and the engines failing to start was not making him happy. Had he been a less religious man, Gavin surely would have been cursing up a storm, even though, alone on the wide, wide ocean hours away from land, no one would have heard him if he did. Instead, turning the key for the fifth time, listening to the engines grind, failing to spring to life, Gavin quietly seethed.

Choosing several tools from a small yellow toolbox located in an aft locker, Gavin began the process of trying to discover what the problem might be. He checked the batteries, electrical connections, everything he could think of but, not being a mechanic, the problem eluded him. A portable VHF radio hung from the control console near the steering wheel. The radio would connect him directly to the tow boat services. He hated to call for help, the indignity of being towed back into port, not to mention the expense. Reluctantly reaching for the VHF radio mic, then pausing mid-reach, he spotted an approaching boat. Amazingly, it was heading right toward him. He waved.

## CHAPTER EIGHT

The boat pulled up alongside *Bite Me*. An eighteen-foot open-bowed water ski boat. What the heck was a boat like that doing way out here?

"Trouble?" the solitary fellow at the controls asked.

"Yeah, thanks for stopping," Gavin replied. "Darndest thing, can't get either engine to start. I was about to radio for help. Glad you came along."

Gavin dropped two white plastic fenders over the gunwale and helped raft the smaller boat to his. The ski boat guy clambered onto the *Bite Me*.

"Gee, this has been such a lucky day for me. Except for the obvious engine trouble. Look at these mahi I caught," Gavin gushed, opening the fish locker, showing off his catch. "And thank the good Lord, you came along just at the right time."

Without warning, the ski boat guy shoved Gavin hard, causing him to fall face first into the locker atop several still-flopping, struggling-for-life mahi mahi, the brilliant colors draining from them, turning slate gray.

"The Lord's got nothin' to do with it, fish face," the man snarled.

Gavin, struggling to turn over onto his back, looking up

at this stranger whom he assumed had come to help. "What the ...?" was all he could muster.

Putting a hand onto Gavin's chest, holding him down, prone atop the fish, bending down to be face-to-face, so close the stranger's heavy dark beard stubble nearly scratching Gavin's own cheek, the stranger held him in this vulnerable position, just staring menacingly. Silence clotted the air between them.

Abruptly releasing his grip on Gavin, he spoke. "Look, maybe it *is* your lucky day after all. I was sent here to kill you. But I don't really wanna kill you. Hell, I don't even know you. So, if you play your cards right, you'll live to see another day."

"What? Who wants you to kill me?" Gavin was beyond incredulous.

The stranger was still glaring, but seemingly considering whether to bother answering the question. "You know some chick named Cantu?"

Gavin shook his head, trying to fathom what he'd just heard. "My wife? Impossible. I don't believe that at all."

This took the stranger aback. "She's your wife? Are you fuckin' kidding me? You're married to her? Jesus!" The stranger then paused briefly. "Believe it! Your wife, the bitch prostitute, sent me. She wants you dead."

"Prostitute? My wife? You're crazy! This is some sort of weird mistake."

"Little Chinese woman, about yay high," said the ski boat guy, holding his free hand about five feet in the air. "Goes by the name of Mistress Cantu."

"Shit," Gavin exhaled. Of course, he knew about her past life in that sinful environ of debauchery. But he was certain that was all in the past. At least he'd been certain until this very moment.

"So, here's what we're gonna do," the ski boat guy began telling him, "I'm gonna slap you around, bruise you up some.

Make you look like you put up a real struggle. Then you're gonna call that wife of yours and tell her to call the police because some guy just attacked you, tried to kill you and steal your boat. But you fought him off and got away. She will not want to call the police, because she knows she's involved. Maybe that will be the end of it. You can both go about living whatever fucked up weirdo lives you must have together."

He paused, watching Gavin listening to his words, absorbing the situation. "Otherwise, I'm gonna break your fuckin' neck right here where you lay and leave you to rot with these damn stinking fish. Got it?"

Gavin nodded.

"You do have a phone on this tub, right?"

Another nod. "But cell coverage way out here is iffy," he added.

"Get it and make the call, right now. I wanna be sure this all pans out. You better fuckin hope the phone works."

Climbing timorously from the fish locker, making his way to the console, picking up his cell phone laying on a shelf, making the call.

"Yes?" he hears his wife's voice.

A momentary feeling of relief that she'd answered, quickly replaced by outrage. "What is going on? There is a man here threatening to kill me! Says you are a prostitute and that you sent him. This guy's one of your whore customers? I married you knowing your horrible sinful past, but this? Th, th, this?" Gavin stammered, struggling for purchase of his thoughts, emotions erupting, shaking his fist at no one. "This guy's the limit! Do you hear me? This guy's the limit!"

"Huh? What you are talking about?" she asked, shocked that her husband was calling her, complicated by difficulty understanding his words over the muffled connection. "The sky's the limit?"

"You're not on script, asshole!" Emsch yells, snatching the phone from Gavin's hand, knocking him down in the process. "Look," now screaming into the phone himself, "I'm here, but I'm not gonna kill him. I rented the fucking motorboat and followed him out here, but that's as far as I go. Whatever weird kinky shit you two got going, count me out. This ain't my brand of freak show. I'm fucking done with you!"

Dead air. Then, "O-kaay, Mistah Emsch," Cantu replied, very slowly, drawing out the vowels. "Yes, Edward Emsch, I know your real name, my sissy. So, you need to understand that if you leave that boat with him still alive, there will magically appear on the internet, before you can even get back to shore, a video of you prancing daintily in your pretty dress, crawling on your knees, licking the soles of my shoes. It will go viral. Your supposedly tough-guy criminal associates will see it. Millions of people everywhere will know the sissy you truly are."

Emsch shuddered involuntarily. The hissing sibilance of her speaking the words *sissy* and pretty *dress* causing both fear and excitement. Looking at the number on the phone and committing it to memory, he shouted ever more loudly, "Fuck you!" Then, complacency settling in. "Fine! You win. I'm lookin' at a dead man."

CHAPTER NINE

# BEN HARDING

Standing there on the beach just outside Vinnie's condo complex, hearing Sammie's voice answering my call, suddenly I wasn't quite sure just what to say to her. Probably not a good idea to just blurt out, "Hi Sammie, I had a mid-life epiphany that you are the love of my life and I intend to pursue you with a vengeance."

"Hello?" I heard her repeat.

I answered, "Hey Sammie. It's me, Ben."

"Oh, Ben. How are you? I love hearing your voice," she responded with an initial familiar sweetness he never found cloying. "But listen, please forgive me, I just can't talk right now. I'm a little overwhelmed." Suddenly more bittersweet, sounding rather frazzled.

"Overwhelmed because you're so excited I called?" I said, levity intended.

A false chuckle, followed by, "You remember my former brother-in-law, Gavin?"

Of course, I did. He was the younger brother of Sammie's

murdered husband. A nice enough guy. Last time I'd seen him he was living in Hawaii with his new bride, a very petite Asian woman named Connie. I remembered them both quite well. I also recalled that Sammie's late husband had been having an affair with that same woman before he died. Then she ends up marrying the brother. Pretty strange stuff.

"Oh Ben, something terrible has happened to Gavin."

"What do you mean?" I asked.

"His wife called. That Connie person. I loathe that conniving bitch, but she sounded really upset. She said Gavin has gone missing. They found his boat out at sea, but he wasn't on it. And he has been gone for over forty-eight hours. I'm scared to death."

"Sammie, that's awful. What can I do to help?"

"Oh Ben, my Ben. You are always there for me. I simply don't know what I would have done without you when my husband died. You helped me so very much. You are my rock. Absolutely. I'm leaving for Hawaii tonight on the red eye. Is there any way you can come too?"

## CHAPTER TEN

# BEN HARDING

Sammie was too worked up to sleep much on the five-and-a-half-hour flight to Honolulu, so we talked most of the way. It was my big chance to tell her how I felt about her, tell her about my epiphany. But I was reluctant to seize the opportunity, once again finding myself in the dilemmic position of consoler-in-chief rather than in some more intimate situation. Instead, we talked about Gavin, his wife, that Samantha had not seen or heard much from them since they moved to Hawaii, and now he was missing.

"I smell foul play here, Ben. I really do. Absolutely. A leopard does not shed its stripes. That woman, Cantu, was a prostitute, she was involved in the death of my husband, Griffin, and now this. Wasn't she even arrested once for attempted murder of some other man?"

"Yes," I answered. "She was charged in Hawaii with attempted murder. A matter of record discovered when you had me investigating her involvement with your husband's death. But she was never convicted." No need for further explanation from me, that Cantu had been engaging in some kinky foreplay with some man when he lost consciousness and was rushed to the hospital. Cantu was arrested but when it was later proven to have been the accidental result of consensual sex, she was acquitted.

"Still. A leopard does not change its stripes," she repeated.

"You mean spots," I corrected. "A leopard has spots, not stripes."

"Whatever." She shrugged. "She is a malicious predator. I just know, deep down in my bones, that she was involved in my husband's death and managed to get off scot-free. I also know that she is now somehow responsible for Gavin's disappearance. He might even be dead. God, Ben! Gavin is probably dead, and that evil woman is somehow responsible. I just know it. I absolutely know it!"

It was the middle of the night when we arrived in Honolulu, a twenty-minute cab ride taking us right to Ala Wai Marina where Gavin and his wife lived on their yacht. I knew exactly where it was located, two docks over from the Hawaii Yacht Club, because I had been there once before back when Gavin and Cantu had first married. If I was expecting some big crime scene with police detectives and blood-sniffing dogs, I was mistaken. Not a soul around.

Connie was, presumably, asleep onboard the yacht. So, I climbed aboard and knocked on an outer door. No answer. I knocked again, much more loudly. She finally answered, not appearing to be too happy for us disturbing her at such an early hour. Motioning for us to follow her inside, sleepily shuffling her way to a rear stateroom inside the capacious yacht, seemingly somnolent, silently pointing to a bed, indicating we should lie down and rest there, then shuffling away, disappearing somewhere toward the front end of the boat.

Sammie and I, both damn tired from not having slept all night, stood staring at the bed for a long moment.

"Just one bed." I said, pointing out the obvious.

"Come on," Sammie replied, pulling me by the arm onto the bed with her. We were both asleep within minutes. I hope I didn't snore.

Sunlight streaming in through a portal window, right into my eyes, woke me up. I looked at my watch: it was nearly noon. That is, it was almost noon in California, I'd not reset my watch to local time. But be it for breakfast or lunch, my stomach was grumbling, reminding me I had not eaten since the meager meal onboard the plane the previous night. I got up, leaving Sammie to sleep, and began giving myself a tour of the yacht, looking for a bathroom and some food. No sign of Cantu. Finding the galley, I began foraging around. Sammie must have heard me, suddenly appearing a few feet away. She smelled of sleep.

"The bathroom?" she asked, groggy.

I pointed toward a tan laminate door a few steps from the galley, "That's the head."

She rolled her eyes and opened the door, disappearing inside.

Just then, Connie made an appearance, shuffling quietly along the cabin floor, barefoot, wearing a muumuu that draped to the floor.

"Good morning," I offered, as cheerfully as I could muster.

"Wha! What you doing here on my boat?" She sounded startled.

"You called Samantha, asked for help. Didn't Sammie tell you we were coming? You were asleep when we arrived. We woke you up. Do you remember letting us onboard?"

"Oh yes, yes. Right," she replied, remembering. "Every morning I must wake up early to see husband go off fishing. Finally, I can sleep late and you two show up before the sun even all da way up. Ugh!"

"Sorry," I offered.

She waved me off. "Don't be sorry. I just grumpy before my morning tea."

I chuckled. She remained stone faced.

"You want coffee or tea?" she asked, rummaging about the galley, pushing me aside.

"Make mine coffee," Sammie said, emerging from the head. "Strong, no cream, no sugar."

Acknowledging that she had heard, Connie then squinted in my direction.

"I'll have the same ... only with cream and sugar ... if you have it."

"Hungry?" Cantu asked, pushing a pink box along the galley countertop in my direction. On the lid were the words *Leonard's Bakery, Home of Malasada and Pao Doce since 1952*. Inside were several pillowy, white, doughy-looking mounds that looked like uncooked dumplings. Also, there were some brownish lumps of dough covered with sugar.

"What are those?" Sammie asked, peering over my shoulder into the box.

"Malasada and manapua," Cantu answered. "Good grinds, fo' sure."

Sammie shrugged.

Cantu grunted at Sammie's apparent ignorance. "Malasadas, *Portugee* fried dough. Much like a doughnut. You will like. And the white ones are manapua. Hawaii's version of char siu bao."

Sammie continued to stare into the box with ambivalence.

"You haoles," Cantu's voice sounding mildly irritated, "manapua are buns filled with Chinese sausage, sweet char siu pork and lup cheong."

We took our coffees and the pink box topside and sat in opposing banquettes around a small ornate table with Chinese symbols on it. The meaty-doughy manapua buns instantly satisfying our morning hunger and the malasadas our sweet tooth. The Hawaiian blue sky overhead, puffy white clouds, gentle trade breeze caressing us, silken, evanescent. This would be a most wonderful morning in paradise, if it were not for the gravitas of why we were assembled here.

"Husband goes fishing almost every morning," Connie Cantu began, absently lighting a slim brown cigarette to go with her tea. Her fingers fidgeted with a square box on the table in front of her, Nat Sherman MCD luxury cigarettes the label read. "He love to fish, fo' sure. Take dat little fishing boat, right there." She was pointing with the cigarette toward the water aft of the yacht, but no fishing boat was to be seen.

"Luxury cigarettes?" I inquired. "I didn't know there was such a thing."

She shrugged. "I like luxury. Luxury smokes, luxury everything."

Sammie, lifting her coffee cup to her lips and softly blowing across the rim, asked, "What fishing boat?"

"Bite Me," she replied.

"Excuse me?" Samie reacted, Cantu's answer sounding somewhere between snide and downright rude.

"Bite Me. That the name of fishing boat. I name it myself," she explained, her lips forming a tight semi-smile.

Sammie and I gave each other a quizzical look. Cantu

noticed. A long draw on the Sherman luxury cigarette, then sighing the smoke outward as if already bored with having to explain. "Oh. It no here right now. Police took it. They found it floating out on da ocean somewhere. They still keeping it."

Of course, the police impounded the boat. It was their only evidence. No body was found. In fact, as Connie continued to explain, the police were still treating this, more or less, as a missing person incident, not yet a full-fledged homicide.

"I'm not getting this," Sammie said, raising her voice an octave. "You sounded totally upset on the phone. Frantic, in fact. But now you don't seem at all upset. And all you can tell me is he went out fishing, just like he does every morning, but this time he didn't return? Did you two have an argument? Were you fighting and maybe that's why he just didn't want to come home? There's got to be something more to this than what you are saying."

Cantu shrugged. "No. We live *pono*."

"Pono?" I asked.

She gave an indignant look while explaining. "Hawaiian. It means living righteous. Very important to people in Hawaii. In fact, it's right there in the state motto: *Ua Mau ke Ea o ka Aina i ka Pono*, and literally translates to *the life of the land is perpetuated in righteousness*."

"So, you and Gavin lived pono? Nothing was wrong in your relationship?"

"I told you. Everything fine, life is very good. Husband love me, husband love to fish, husband disappear. That is whole story." Pausing, then adding, "Of course I was upset when I called you. It had just happened. I call you right after I call HPD. Police tell me to stay calm. How I can stay calm? My husband not come home. He always comes home. Always! So, I call you. Gotta call somebody."

"The police did conduct a search for him though?" I asked rhetorically because the answer appeared obvious. "That's how they found the boat? The one they impounded?"

"That is correct," Cantu answered. "I was screaming at them to find my husband, to find Gavin. They finally sent search boats looking for him, I think just to appease me. I really think they thought he was just out having an affair, or getting drunk, like some husbands do. But Gavin not like that. You both know him. You both know Gavin not do stuff like dat."

Sammie and I exchanged glances. It was true. Neither drunkenness nor an affair comported with the Gavin we knew.

"But they searched," Cantu continued. "And when all they found was his empty boat, dat did scared me even more. Gavin is probably gone forever. He must have fallen overboard and drowned." Another long drag on the skinny brown Sherman, then adding, "Or eaten by sharks. Why else would boat be found but no Gavin, so far out at sea, so many miles away? No man can survive. Unless some miracle, Gavin is with his Lord now. This is what I feel. This is why I am more calm now. Sad, but calm."

"We need to go to the police," Sammie told me, leaning close, sotto voce, when Connie excused herself to go below and get more tea. "There's got to be more to all this than what she is telling us. That is the most *insincere sincere* woman I have ever known. I need more info. You're a lawyer, you can get the police to tell us what we want to know."

"Unless I'm representing a client, being a lawyer gets me nothing with the police," I told her. "Not to mention, I am just a civilian here. I'm not a licensed attorney in Hawaii."

"Still," she insisted, "you know the right way to deal with them."

We borrowed Connie's car, a cream-colored Mercedes, to drive over and pay a visit to the Honolulu Police Department. "This car gives me the creeps," Sammie remarked with a visible shudder. "Like, it contains some sort of diseased karmic energy or something." She sat looking out the passenger-side window, glumly watching Waikiki go by. "My dear late husband bought this car for her. Probably with money that was half mine. Never in my wildest imagination would I have dreamed that my husband would be sleeping with some whore, buying her an expensive car, and that someday I'd be riding in it … here in Hawaii no less, on my way to the police station."

I thought she was done venting, but she went on.

"This is where the shoe really pinches. First my husband buys her this damn car, then he dies, and she marries his brother, and now, here I am in the damn car. And what is the common denominator in all this? That evil Chinese woman! It cannot be just coincidence that she was involved in both Griffin's death and now Gavin's disappearance as well. I feel like I'm driving around and around a cul-de-sac that never gets me anywhere but I keep seeing her at each completed circle."

"Calm down," I suggested. "You can't just be jumping to conclusions. Weird stuff happens all the time. Someone could just as easily point out that *your* very presence indicates that you are involved in both incidents as well. Or even that I am involved in both incidents."

"Oh Ben, that's such nonsense. I'm not evil. But she really is. I'm convinced of at least that much. And, as for you, I am the one who has involved you, both times. Your only involvement is through the goodness of your heart. And I do appreciate it. Absolutely."

The local police refused to give us any information, other than it was an ongoing investigation. They took our names and contact info, as part of some general report I'm certain, and sent us on our way. "Another damn cul-de-sac," Sammie muttered as we left the police station.

CHAPTER ELEVEN

Sometimes he hated leaving Oahu. Hated to leave the blissful calm of the island, palm trees and hula girls swaying with the rhythm of gentle trade-winds, the aroma of plumeria permeating the air; hated returning to the reality of home on the California mainland. This was *not* one of those times, however. This time Eddy Emsch was more than happy to be landing at LAX and leaving all that island stuff behind. After all the crap he'd been involved with on this last visit, he was pretty sure it would be a long, long time before he showed his face there again. If ever.

Home, a two-hour drive from L.A., in the rural regions of the Temecula Valley, was its own sort of coveted paradise. Relaxed now in his S Class Mercedes, homeward bound, driving along the two-lane Rancho California Road, sunroof open to allow in the full aromatic splendor permeating from acres of orange trees, equally as intoxicating as Oahu's plumeria, felt like returning to a perfectly delightful reality.

Where the orange groves stopped, endless acres of grapevines began. Passing dozens of wineries with Tuscan-style buildings dotting the hills, he knew he was a lucky man to be living in such a California paradise. Screw Hawaii, who needs that place?

A few turns off the main road, passing an ancient weathered yellow farmhouse, then onto a dirt road leading to a partially paved single lane of blacktop, and finally slowing to a rolling stop at an elaborate wrought iron gate festooned with a sculpted metal cowboy riding a horse whilst holding a basket of grapes. Above the gate, scrolled lettering: *Paniolo Rose Winery*. Pushing a button under the car's rear-view mirror, gates began opening. A quick sigh before pressing on the accelerator and motoring up a long winding driveway, putting Hawaii and all that had transpired there on this last visit in his rear-view mirror. Up, up, up, stopping in front of the familiar white framed Southern plantation style house he called home. He was glad to be back.

It was Eddy's wife who first had the dream of moving to the Temecula Valley Wine Country a dozen years ago. They had driven out from Los Angeles for a weekend of wine tasting at the more than forty wineries spread out over the valley, and his new bride, Rosie, completely fell in love with the area. Eddy didn't really care a whit about wine, he was more of a beer guy – or perhaps scotch, depending on his mood – but the uniqueness of the Old Town section of downtown Temecula with its colorful history and old buildings dating back to the 1800s, and the overall sort of Old West cowboy flare, appealed to him.

"I really want to move here," Rosie announced as they headed in the car back to Los Angeles after a perfectly delightful weekend. "It's like a dream place. Like Napa, only local and with more sun."

At first Eddy balked at the idea, it was such a remote spot. Too far from everything. But he quickly realized its remoteness could actually be an asset ... and getting into the wine business might prove an excellent cover for his shadier drug business dealings.

Not three months later they purchased thirty-six acres of

rolling hillside in what Eddy referred to as the middle of nowhere and began building, at the highest point of the property, their six-thousand square foot dream house, designed by Rosie, with a view that was nothing short of spectacular. On a clear day they could see all the way to the ocean, roughly thirty-five miles as the crow flies, out in the distance.

Much like the famous French wine regions that include the great hill of Hermitage, where powerful Syrah dominate production, and in the northern Rhône, the Condrieu AOP, which provides the world with luxurious and aromatic Viognier wines, Temecula's granitic soil is known to be ideal for production of similar wines. So, shortly after moving in, the planting of grapes began – viognier, a white grape, as well as some red varieties, such as Syrah, Grenache, and Cinsault. They christened their new home The Paniolo Rose Winery – paniolo being the Hawaiian word for cowboy, which Eddy decided suited him because of his love of the Islands while factoring in the Wild West theme of the historic Temecula Old Town; and Rose for the winery's founder, Rosie Emsch.

The problem with Temecula, however, is that it was often regarded by many in the industry as the bastard sibling to its more well-known sister wine areas farther to the north. It was not well known enough to sustain distribution to the general markets nationwide. Temecula wineries, therefore, mostly make money by catering to the three-million-plus visitors from Los Angeles, San Diego, and surrounding areas that come to visit for the day, taste the offerings from the various vintners, and perhaps purchase some of the wines they enjoyed to take home with them. Because of that, Rosie decided to build a beautiful out-building to be used as a tasting room to accommodate the public. Their business soon became profitable.

But it was Rosie's dream to have her wines sold in other

markets and in restaurants around the West and to expand with other related products, such as locally produced olive oil. So, they also created Paniolo Rose Olive Oil Company. Toward that end, Eddy had begun traveling to other states to promote Paniolo Rose products. Some modicum of success had been achieved and they were now featured on many restaurant menus and in stores around the Western U.S. In the process, he embraced an ever-increasing fondness for Hawaii and returned often under the guise of marketing those products to Island restaurants and shops. But this last trip had demanded something far more and, he knew, it would be his final visit to the land of aloha.

## CHAPTER TWELVE

# BEN HARDING

Gavin remained missing. Two months and nine days elapsed since his disappearance. It remained an open police case and ongoing investigation in Hawaii. Samantha was growing more and more certain of two things: that Gavin was no longer among the living and that his wife, Connie Cantu, was somehow responsible.

Sammie sat across the table from me sipping a huge margarita at our favorite local Mexican restaurant, Baja Cantina, opining with absolute certainty on those two facts and how she felt so helpless to bring any sort of justice to Gavin's likely demise. A dark-haired waitress in low-cut peasant blouse and short ruffled skirt placed our food on the table in front of us: triple tacos for Sammie and a super large steaming beef burrito with rice and beans for me.

"My god, that is enormous," Sammie giggled, shaking her head and pointing to my plate. "How the hell do you not get fat? If I ate that my ass would no longer fit in this chair. I swear. Absolutely."

"Forty Miles of Bad Road is what they call it on the menu, but I've had it before and it's all good road, believe me," I answered. I was about to fork into it when I spotted Vinnie Scatucci entering the restaurant.

"Scatucci!" I shouted, waving my fork in the air. "Come on over and join us."

Still in office attire, dark blue suit, necktie loosened, he sauntered in our direction, sitting himself down onto a decorative wooden chair between Sammie and me. Instantly the waitress reappeared, all smiles, offering him a menu. From his seated position, looking up at her, Scatucci took a slow appreciative survey of her long legs, narrow waist, and cleavage. Finally settling on her face, returning her smile with a devilishly charming one I've seen him use so often, waving off the menu, told her, "Just drinks for me, sweetie." Pointing to Sammie's margarita, Scatucci added, "Bring me one of those. I'll take it with Cruz Del Sol Tequila if you have it."

"Of course, sir," the waitress replied, still all smiles.

"And put whatever my friends here are having on my tab, will ya doll?"

Sweetie? Doll? Scatucci always managed to sound strangely suave, when talk like that from most guys would come off downright cheesy. She flashed a highly flirtatious look his way, "*El placer es mio, señor.*" Then trotted away with short mincing steps.

Scatucci and Sammie had not met before, so I introduced them. "Vinnie here is a criminal lawyer. He's the one you might want to complain to about injustice."

"Just your everyday household drug dealers and madams, those are my specialties," he joked.

"Yes, yes. I remember seeing you on television a long time ago. On the evening news. That big case involving drugs and a big-time car manufacturer," Sammie said.

"Yes, thank you. Such a memory you have. That was a rather complicated case. The police used entrapment to trick my client into doing a criminal act he would not otherwise have done. Happily, I was able to bring about justice for a man who otherwise might have gone to prison."

Sammie began telling Scatucci the story of Gavin's mysterious disappearance. Scatucci's attentive listening got briefly interrupted by the waitress' arrival with his margarita.

"Thank you," Vincent said, turning from Samantha to look toward the woman now standing next to him holding a tray with his drink. His gaze evolving to a deep-seated sustained audit of the server's facial features. "You know," Scatucci said thoughtfully, looking deep into her eyes, "you look like you might have a little Italian in you."

"I don't think so," she responded.

"Hmm," Scatucci quipped, "well, would you like a little?"

"Oh you," she said, blushing, giggling. "I should have seen that coming."

Sammie's jaw dropped at such alarming inappropriateness. She shot me a look of instant disapproval. I shrugged my shoulders, shaking my head in disbelief. If I would have said such a thing, the woman would likely have thrown a drink in my face but, coming from Scatucci, she just laughs. Go figure.

From the look Sammie had given me, I felt it was my place to say something of admonishment. After all, he was *my* friend who I invited to join us. "Um, Vinnie, I don't think men are allowed to make jokes like that anymore."

"Like what?" he asked, taking a sip from his glass. He had no clue. I left it there.

With the food server gone, Sammie resumed her original oration of the events, as she knew them, involving Gavin's disappearance, shaking off her outrage over the sexist joke, or perhaps merely shelving it for the moment. Scatucci listened, appearing genuinely interested, shaking his head sympathetically, interrupting her at times with questions, and offering a few legal caveats along the way. I was glad to see Sammie unloading on someone besides me. I had heard it all before and had nothing new to really offer her.

"It's a frustrating process," Vinnie told her in conclusion. "But you have to be patient. Let the police do their job. When they nail it all down, let the lawyers prosecute and defend. Without the law it's all just darkness." That seemed to appease her, if only momentarily.

The topic of conversation then shifted to other less weighty matters and Sammie found an opportunity to raise her objection about Scatucci's so-called joke, making it clear that she had found it to be offensive. Scatucci looked genuinely surprised. "I am so sorry," he replied with what appeared absolute sincerity. "I don't know why I say things like that. Maybe it's the company I keep."

Sammie gave him a look with raised eyebrows.

"Oh no, there I did it again, didn't I? I don't mean *present* company. I meant my clients. You know? The aforementioned druggies and ladies of the night? That is their sort of humor, and it just rubs off on me I'm afraid."

Samantha's look of rigidity remained.

"Of course, you are right," he conceded. "When the waitress returns, I will certainly apologize."

As we were finishing our meals, and Vinnie drained the final drops from his margarita, the server came by to see if there was anything else we might need.

"*Gracias. Solo la cuenta, por favor,*" Scatucci responded in Spanish with a distinct Detroit intonation, adding, "By the way, please allow me to apologize for the inappropriateness of my stupid attempt at humor earlier. It was offensive and I'm very sorry." He paused, waiting for some response from her. When none was forthcoming, he added, "I will stop talking now, lest I say something further that is consistent with my tawdry personality."

She just smiled without any indication of emotion. As she retreated, I wondered if she was secretly angry.

"Did not know you speak Spanish," I commented after she left.

"Some of my clients over the years did not speak much English, so I learned."

The waitress returned a few moments later with the check. Scatucci picked it up, smiled, and showed it to me. The waitress had written her phone number on the bill, with a note that read: *If there's anything else you need that is consistent with your personality, give me a call.*

CHAPTER THIRTEEN

An interesting series of events began taking place regarding the disappearance of Gavin Gambil. Other than the fact that he appeared to be missing from a small boat in the middle of the Pacific, which in and of itself was certainly suspicious, there was no tangible sign of foul play. No blood. No damage to the boat. No body. The Honolulu police, however, did find fingerprints on Gavin's boat belonging to an Edward Emsch of California, prompting an interstate investigation that led to the wine country of Temecula, specifically to a location called Paniolo Rose Vineyards. It was at that location that Eddy Emsch was first questioned by the authorities.

Officers Kardon and Harman were at the front gate. Rosie buzzed them in then, walking out the front door of the house, waited for their car to traverse the steep driveway.

"Geez, check out the greeter," Kardon remarked to Harman, as the car came to a stop. "That is one very classy looking lady."

Extending her hand, Rosie introduced herself in a lilting voice met only by stifled pleasantry. The officers showed their identifications and with sober tones said they would like to speak to her husband. Perplexed, she invited them inside, bid them to take a seat in the spacious living room, then went upstairs to get her husband.

"What's this all about?" she asked Eddy. He was in the process of getting dressed, pulling on a clean shirt, buttoning buttons.

"Nothing for you to worry about, my love. Maybe somebody's suing us or something. You never know what might happen when you own a successful business. People wanna mess with ya. You stay up here. I'll take care of this."

Eddy came downstairs wondering what it was that could have led the police to his door. Though, at the forefront of his mind, he worried it had something to do with his involvement with that crazy bitch in Hawaii and her equally crazy husband.

The officers' line of questioning seemed innocent enough at first. If they had any real evidence of anything criminal they wouldn't be asking such insipid questions, Eddy figured. So, he decided to answer all of their questions truthfully, if possible, since that was easier than trying to remember a series of untruths after the fact.

Then Officer Harman asked if Emsch had been to Hawaii in the last several months?

He answered cautiously. Yes, he'd gone there on business.

What sort of business did he conduct in Hawaii?

Trying to sell our Temecula wine and our line of olive oil to retailers and restaurants on Oahu, to be sold under a Hawaiian name and label.

Can you supply us with the names of any of those Hawaiian businesspeople you met with?

Absolutely, no problem at all. I can get them to you.

Where did you stay while in Hawaii?

The Hilton Hawaiian Village at Waikiki.

This went on for an hour or more, Officer Kardon remaining silent throughout Officer Harman's questioning, as if quietly making mental notes of it all.

When it seemed as if the questioning had finally run its course, Officer Harman finally spoke up, asking, "Did you meet with, or happen to even know in any way, a resident of Oahu by the name of Gavin Gambil?"

Without hesitation, Emsch replied, "No. That name does not sound like anyone I ever met over there. Most of the people I met with had Asian surnames or long voweled Hawaiian names." The answer was truthful. Eddy did not know the actual name of the man on the boat he was sent to kill, or if that was even who they were referring to.

"You're not a fisherman, by any chance, are you Mr. Emsch?"

Okay, now the questioning was turning from insipid to extremely pertinent. Small beads of perspiration began forming on Emsch's forehead. "I don't fish. I don't even like the water, other than being on shore, maybe, just looking out at it. Hardly ever even eat fishy things. Can't stand the smell."

"Too bad," Officer Harman added, smiling. "Me? I'm a diehard angler. Love to fish."

"To each his own, I guess," Eddy said, instantly regretting such a terse response.

"These folks you met with over there, the ones with the Asian names. Any of them women?"

"Actually, no. If memory serves, they were all men."

"You never met with a woman? A woman named Gambil? Connie Gambil?"

Emsch shook his head. "I already told you no. Gambil? That's not Asian or Hawaiian, and most of my meetings were with people with Asian and Hawaiian names."

"Oh, right. Yes, sorry. Just to be clear, though. You never met up with a woman by the name of ..." Harman stopped abruptly as if trying to recall the woman's name, looking over at the other officer for assistance.

"Cantu," Kardon, the other officer supplemented, suddenly chiming in.

"Yes, that's right. Sometimes she goes by the last name of Cantu. You never met with a woman named Cantu? Connie Cantu?"

Emsch swallowed hard. Shaking his head slowly in a negative non-verbal response, finding himself venturing silently into the untruthful category, as Officer Harman continued.

"She's Asian. Chinese, I believe. Asian *and* Hawaiian."

Emsch still shaking his head, sweat beads accumulating on his forehead.

"Lives on a great big old yacht in the marina? Right near to the hotel where you say you were staying?"

Emsch finally managing to verbalize a response, "Sorry. Chinese, Japanese, they all look more-or-less alike to me. I know, I know, you're not supposed to say things like that these days, but it's true. I can't tell one from another. Maybe *they* feel the same about us non-Asians, can't tell one of us from another. Who knows? At any rate, I don't recall meeting any woman with that name."

Harman looked purposefully over at Kardon. Kardon looked back.

"This is beginning to feel kinda weird. Do I need a lawyer?" Emsch spoke out.

"That's up to you, Mr. Emsch. Completely up to you if you think you need a lawyer. We're not necessarily accusing you of anything unlawful. All we're trying to do here is to understand why your fingerprints were found on a boat in Hawaii, a boat belonging to a Mr. Gavin Gambil."

"I have no idea," Emsch responded, perhaps a bit too quickly.

"Mr. Gambil has gone missing," Harman added.

"Missing how?"

"That's what we were hoping you might be able to help us answer. I mean, your fingerprints were all over that boat. I was hoping you might have some answers for us. Help in some small way to solve the mystery of his disappearance. But your answers here today only seem to be compounding that mystery."

"I don't know how I can give you answers if I don't have any."

Harman sighed audibly. "Okay. Look, you have a really beautiful home here. I mean, this house, the view outside … owning a winery for gosh sake. The stuff of dreams. And that wife of yours who let us in? A real stunner, for sure. And she seems really nice. A cultured, sophisticated lady. You seem to be an exceptionally lucky man, Mr. Emsch. So, I'm gonna level with you. This whole thing is just not adding up for me."

"What's not adding up?" Emsch asked nervously, but genuinely confused.

"This guy Gambil in Hawaii goes out fishing on his boat, then goes missing out at sea. Did some sort of misfortune befall him? Of course, it did. But was it accidental or murder? First thing we did was, we interviewed Ms. Cantu, his wife. That shed no light on the situation. Then your fingerprints were found on the boat. We interviewed Ms. Cantu again. Know what she told us, Mr. Emsch?"

"I have no idea, because I have no idea who this Cantu person is," Emsch replied, deciding it was now better to flat out lie.

"She told us an interesting story about how you and her were having an affair."

"She said what?" Eddy was stunned.

"I know. Listen, after seeing that wife of yours, I gotta admit, I really don't get it. When you got *that* here at home, why would you wanna cheat with this Hawaiian gal. But be that as it may, her story is that you and her were having an affair. Hooking up each time you came to Hawaii on business. That you became obsessed with her. That you told her you could not live without her."

"What!" Eddy was incredulous.

"That's when she broke it off with you. She told you she was never going to leave her husband. And that is when you threatened to kill her husband."

"That's insane!" Eddy shouted, a mixture of confusion, surprise, and rage in his voice.

"Well, that's why I said it just doesn't quite add up for me, either. So, would you like to revise your answers and tell me the real story? You do know this woman, correct?"

Eddy hesitated several long moments before answering. He wasn't quite sure how to begin. How on earth could he explain to these policemen the relationship he had been having with Cantu?

"Yes, okay. I do know her, but it wasn't at all like that," he reluctantly confessed. "We were not having any sort of affair and I certainly was never in love with that woman. I mean, get serious. She's a ..." he searched for words, "a madam, a pro." Emsch took a deep breath before clarifying. "A madam who caters to certain ... oh how can I put this? She caters to men with certain kinky fetishes. There was nothing serious going on. I was just a guy away from home having fun."

"That's the trouble with trouble. It always starts out as fun," Harman commented, shaking his head simpatico.

Emsch inferred from Harman shaking his head that he was expected to continue.

"She was the only madam I knew in Hawaii, so yes, I did contact her on many of my business trips there. She satisfied a certain, shall we say, *need*," Eddy explained, making curly quotes with his fingers at the word need.

The officers remained motionless, unexpressive.

"Come on, we're all guys here," Emsch pleaded. "You must know what I'm talking about."

He detected a slight smile at the corners of Harman's lips.

Encouraged, Emsch continued. "I wasn't lying when I said I didn't know this Gavin Gambil person. She never told me his name. Never even told me he was her husband. Just that she wanted me to mess with the guy a little. Wanted me to shake him up for her. At first, I thought it was just some sort of weird kinky shit she and him were into. That she wanted me to fuck with him somehow. I thought maybe that was somehow his thing. You know, something he was into. I told her she was nuts, to count me out. Too kinky for me."

"So, how did your prints get on the boat?"

"She had a way of ... I know this sounds crazy, but she had a way of convincing me to do certain things. I can't fuckin' explain it. She convinced me to do something to the boat so that it would conk out after a couple hours. So, I did. I messed with his boat. I figured even if it did conk out on the ocean, he could just radio for help. Get rescued by the Coast Guard or something."

"What else did she *convince* you to do?" Harman asked, mimicking Emsch by using curly fingers to air quote the word "convince."

"Nothing else," Emsch lied, fearing he had already said too much, not wanting to divulge any further information regarding his involvement. "That's all I did. I just figured it was all a part of some kinky shit they were doing. And now you tell me he was her husband, so I guess the boat that she had me mess with was half hers. Hawaii's a community property state, isn't it? Like California? I mean, her asking me to mess up a boat that she actually half-owned herself can't be illegal, right? But the whole crazy scenario convinced me to cut ties with that crazy broad. I came home and vowed to myself never to contact her again."

A few more questions and they were done. The police officers politely thanked Eddy for his cooperation, and they left. Eddy watched the unmarked cop car exit out the gate at the bottom of the hill, walked back inside and closed the door behind him before plopping himself onto an oversized ersatz leather chair in the room where he'd just been questioned. Using his shirt tail to mop beads of sweat from his damp brow, he sat transfixed for several minutes, trying to sort out in his mind what had just transpired. Suddenly it all made sense. Rosie entered the room and heard him chuckling to himself.

"What's so amusing, my love?"

"Apparently, it is not a criminal act to fuck up the motor of a boat at the owner's request," he told her.

She didn't understand his humor, asking lightheartedly, "What are you talking about?"

He laughed. "Oh nothing. Long story. Strange notions just amuse me, I guess."

Rosie raised an eyebrow.

"How's about picking out a nice bottle from the cellar?" he suggested. "I feel a small celebration may be in order. Oh, and grab me a beer too, if ya don't mind. I need something cold to wet my whistle after answering all those questions. Then I'll start on the wine."

CHAPTER FOURTEEN

For Connie Cantu, it was the best of facts, it was the worst of facts. Because Gavin's body had not actually been found, the life insurance company would not pay out. Additionally, Gavin's bank accounts were in his name alone. Without a death certificate, Connie was unable to gain access to the accounts. The paltry checking account in both their names would not last long. Paying monthly bills, including the slip fee for her floating home, was a struggle.

On the other hand, there was no actual murder without a body. This was still a missing person case. But the police were still sniffing around. Did they somehow suspect her? Connie wondered what her sissy slave Emsch might have blabbed, leading the cops to suspect her. Several times the police had shown up importuning her with pointed questions. It was a frightening experience and she tried to put on a brave face when answering.

"I have *da kine* alibi witnesses who can testify dat I was all alone the entire day Gavin go missing," she informed them adamantly.

"And how is that possible Mrs. Gambil?"

"What you mean?" she asked.

"How is it possible to have been all alone and have witnesses?"

"Well, I do," she insisted.

The officers looked toward each other, rolling their eyes. "Maybe it would be better for you to come to the station to discuss this further."

"Correct me if I am wrong but don't I have a Constitutional right to make phone call first?" she asked with a demanding tone.

"Constitutional right?" one of the officers replied. "Ma'am, I don't think there were phones when the Constitution was written."

Obviously, they had no real evidence against her, but she could sense their suspicions. So, she decided to turn the tables. Shift the suspicion back to big mouth Emsch by informing the police about his illegal drug business and his criminal connections.

"Edward Emsch loved me," she insisted. "He love me in so many kinda ways, some dat were quite alarming actually. He had such strange desires. Very strange. And he very scary. A bad man. I am good Christian woman, married to good Christian man. Ask anyone who know my husband, they will tell you what a God-fearing man he is. Was. Lord, I don't even know what tense to use when talking about him, whether he alive or dead. But I can tell you I suffered greatly from the guilt of allowing myself to become associated with the likes of Mistah Emsch, associated in a way that violated my spousal vows to my dear, loving husband. I prayed to Jesus every day and night for the strength to end my illicit relationship with Edward Emsch. But he hard man to break away from. And wen I told him I would never leave my husband, that wen I grew very afraid something like this would happen. But I could not warn husband without disclosing my terrible affair. I could not bear the thought of my darling Gavin thinking of me as some horrible cheating wife.

There can be no doubt that Edward Emsch did something to Gavin. Emsch is a criminal. He smuggle drugs in and out through his wine business in California. He told me all about it, many times, boasting about his friends and his connections with drug lords in places like Columbia and South America. I tell you, he very scary man."

## CHAPTER FIFTEEN

The tip Cantu offered the authorities was that, while Paniolo Rose Winery was shipping bottles of their wine to consumers all over the state of California and beyond, not all the shipments contained actual wine. Cocaine, liquidized cocaine, was being shipped from the vineyard in wine bottles and transported in unmarked trucks.

For the two Federal agents who had been assigned to observing the daily activities at the winery, this was all they had to go on. And so far, all they saw was what appeared to be normal business operations, shipments of wine leaving the vineyard. Trucks arrived and trucks departed. Then, on one particular day, they noticed something different. Nothing suspicious about it at first, except that one of the trucks was unmarked, differing from the other trucks entering and exiting the vineyard on any given day. The other trucks bore markings of legitimate trucking companies, logos, phone numbers posted prominently on the trucks. This one was strikingly plain. But it conformed with the information they had received about a drug operation originating from this facility.

So, they stopped the unmarked truck and strong-armed the driver into letting them inspect the cargo. Several dozen wooden boxes were inside, leaving much of the remaining cargo area unoccupied. Each box was labeled FRAGILE WINE PRODUCT. Without further consent from the driver, one of the agents jumped into the rear cargo area, randomly selected a box, and pried it open.

"What ya got?" the other agent, standing outside the truck with the driver, asked.

"Looks like wine bottles," came the reply. "Big bottles." Pulling a bottle from the box, holding it up for the other agent to see.

"Magnums, those big bottles are called magnums," the agent told him. "Looks like they might even be double-magnums."

"This wine any good?" the agent holding the bottle asked the driver.

The driver shrugged.

"I don't know if I've ever tasted really good wine," the agent went on. "I think this looks like some good stuff, what with this big bottle and all. Maybe we should give it a little taste. Hey Rubin," he shouted to the other agent, "you got a corkscrew?"

"As a matter of fact, I just happen to have one right here in my pocket. Never leave home without it," the second agent replied, producing a Swiss Army knife, sliding out a corkscrew attachment from within the red handle, and handing it to his fellow agent.

The cork came out easily. Probably too easily. And that's when the agent noticed an unusual chemical odor from the contents of the bottle and a thick syrup-like consistency of the so-called wine. "I'm no wine expert, but I don't think this stuff smells or looks like wine," he reported to the agent still outside the truck alongside the driver.

Indeed, it was not vino. The confiscated shipment subsequently tested positive for liquid cocaine. Cocaine smuggled in liquid form, with the right refinement system at its final distribution point, could be turned back into powder form through a recrystalization process. Each magnum bottle contained around twelve pounds of liquidized cocaine. Each bottle with an estimated street value of approximately $350,000. Based upon the yields per bottle and number of bottles seized, maybe 260 pounds of cocaine, the entire seized shipment was worth well over twenty million dollars. An excellent day's work for the two Federal agents who made the bust. A very bad day for Eddy Emsch.

In short order, a whole team of government officers, detectives, and drug sniffing canines intruded upon the normally tranquil setting of Paniolo Rose Winery, turning the daily operations to chaos. Opening barrels, opening bottles, searching through chai rooms, silos, storage facilities ... and finding absolutely nothing to tie Emsch to a drug operation.

Rose Emsch was beyond outrage. This invasion into her otherwise quiet, orderly life was incomprehensible. She looked to Eddy for solace but found none. The officers questioned her, alleging involvement in some sort of illegal activities as part of her wine business that she just could not quite comprehend. She was mortified, reduced to tears. In a separate room, Eddy was questioned. In the end, nothing specifically incriminating had been discovered. However, Eddy's laptop computer, as well as Rose's, were confiscated.

The following day, the officers returned. This time taking Eddy into custody for, as Rose saw it, no good reason. Putting her husband in the unmarked police car, they drove away, leaving Rose in a state of utter confusion.

Seated on a hard metal chair in a stark interrogation room, Eddy swallowed hard as he was confronted with the facts against him. Serious allegations. Liquid cocaine discovered in wine bottles bearing his winery labels, and in a truck leaving his winery. Serious charges of his involvement in an illegal drug operation.

An hour or more passed. Eddy grew more than weary from the questioning, his head hurting from the constant mental barrage, finding it difficult to stay focused. Then, abruptly, the line of questioning inexplicably shifted gears.

"Connie Cantu," he heard one of the officers say, without segue. "Let's talk about her for a bit. And the disappearance of a Mr. Gavin Gambil."

It startled him. How did this fit in with the drug charges?

Email correspondence between Connie Cantu and Emsch had been found on his laptop. How they discovered the emails was a mystery, because Eddy had deleted all references to Mistress Cantu.

Intense questioning continued. "There's enough here to prove your involvement in the disappearance of Mr. Gambil," an officer finally flat out told him. "If he turns up dead, you're looking at murder charges, not just drug smuggling."

"I swear I never harmed that guy in any way. All I did was cause his boat engine to malfunction. How many times do I have to tell you guys? How many different ways do I have to say it?"

It began to seem to Eddy that his involvement in Gambil's disappearance was being used against him primarily as leverage to get information on the cocaine operation. Threatening potential murder charges to scare him. At some point, Eddy began thinking if he just cooperated regarding the drug charges, perhaps he could cut some sort of deal, avoid any sort of murder rap. So he caved, giving them the operational overview of his involvement, plus names of people involved in the drug operation, including the name Rojas Raton. The mention of that name causing the interrogating officer to sit up in his chair. Suddenly, another officer entered the room, appearing out of nowhere. They wanted to hear all about it.

Getting cocaine and other illegal drugs into the United States was a problem long ago resolved by those in the business. Finding innovative ways of distributing the illegal products throughout the U.S. was more challenging. Emsch was one of several distributors enlisted, with some mild coercion, to become a part of the distribution chain. Emsch began as a very minor player. Initially, it was just a side hustle for easy extra money. Then he was dragged deeper into the drug business by a South American investor who made cheap money available for Emsch to use to buy and develop the winery. Cheap money, but with some strings attached. Once the winery was up and running, the investor, who Emsch identified to the police as Rojas Raton, muscled his way into the Temecula operation and began using it as a method of illegal distribution.

Cocaine went easily from Columbia to the U.S./Mexico border, then crossing into the States via elaborate tunneling systems, and loaded onto trucks just outside San Diego. The hour-long truck route from San Diego to Temecula proved geographically workable. The rural setting and legitimacy of a wine business sealed the deal. Cocaine arrived by truck, was transferred to bottles and even barrels labeled as wine, and exited the winery by truck, to be delivered to outlets all over the Western United States. And Rojas Raton, a Columbian national currently living in San Diego, had long been a person of interest to the authorities. This was big!

## CHAPTER SIXTEEN

# BEN HARDING

Maybe a month or so after I'd run into Vincent Scatucci at the Baja Cantina, I ran into him again. This time at the Cow's End, a Bohemian-style coffee bar located a block off the Venice Pier. I was in line ordering my morning java and noticed him seated nearby reading the sports section of the LA Times and sipping from a large mug made to look like a baseball. A self-proclaimed sports addict, baseball was his favorite game. "In high school I lettered in baseball," he once told me. "My dream would be to play on a pro team if I would'a had the talent. Unfortunately for me, I didn't. So here I am, a lawyer. Not a bad second choice, I guess."

Coffee in hand, I walked over and sat myself down onto a brightly colored chair with fabric depicting surfing cows holding coffee mugs, located directly across from him. Sunglasses resting atop a head of artfully disheveled hair, he was wearing a black Tommy Bahama shirt, dark linen slacks, and expensive-looking Italian braided loafers with no socks. A two-toned gold/stainless

Rolex was strapped loosely to his wrist, dangling like a bracelet. Casual but pricey attire worn with sartorial flair. When he didn't look up, I remarked, "No suit today. Day off?"

Lifting his eyes from the newspaper in his lap and flashing that charismatic Scatucci smile, "Hey *paesan*. What'cha up to?"

"Same old, same old," I answered. "Just the start of another boring day in paradise."

"I hear ya," he concurred. "Hey, feel like a change of scenery? If you got nothin' planned, I'm driving out to wine country to interview a new client. Come on with me. I could use the company. We can go do a few wine places afterward. Tip some local vino."

"Napa or Santa Ynez? Either way, dude, that's a long drive."

"No and no. The closer wine country. Opposite direction. Down by San Diego. Temecula."

"When?"

"Soon as I drain this mug & finish with the paper."

"Sure. Why not? Just let me run home and put some clothes on. Board shorts and flips probably aren't appropriate for cruising out to wine country."

"I'll pick you up at your place in fifteen minutes," he said.

The top was off Scatucci's red Ferrari. The noise of the wind and whining engine made for shouted conversation as we sped southward along the 15 freeway. Scatucci was telling me about this new client, the one we were now on our way to see. I couldn't quite hear every word, but the gist was that this guy had been arrested on drug charges, part of some big illegal drug operation, accused of using his wine business as a cover. He kept referring to him as Emsch. I figured it was some sort of drug slang, but finally asked, "So, what the hell is an Emsch? Sounds like a character out of The Hobbit or a Harry Potter novel."

Scatucci thought that was pretty funny. "It's his name. Eddy Emsch. I got him out on bail. He's not supposed to leave his house, so I'm coming to him."

Exiting the freeway, onto a highway, turning off on some winding two-lane roads, passing avocado groves, orange groves, acres of vineyards, eventually stopping at ornate iron gates adorned with the scrolled words: Paniolo Rose Winery. The gates opened. We drove up a rather steep hill, the Ferrari engine whining louder as Scatucci shifted gears.

Before we had even gotten out of the car, a strikingly beautiful woman walked out of the house to greet us. Classy, feminine. No discernable make-up, dressed in a simple white blouse and jeans, making denim look as upscale as an evening gown. Slender wrists from which several bracelets dangled. She was tall, wearing flats, still slightly taller than Scatucci and myself. She seemed upset, standoffish, maybe even a little scared. Who wouldn't be, I suppose, when your spouse has just been arrested for various felonies? Scatucci flashed his infamous smile her way. She appeared to soften a tad.

Scatucci and Mr. Emsch conferred in private in Mr. Emsch's study. I'm a lawyer, but I'm not a criminal defense lawyer and Emsch was not my client. Whatever he had to tell Scatucci was none of my business. My very presence could destroy the attorney/client privilege. Mrs. Emsch led me outside, around to the back of the house, where we sat at poolside under a shady copse and chatted.

I remarked about the view, which was truly amazing. She indulged me several minutes of sitting silently, taking in the endless rolling hills of grapevines under a cobalt blue sky. It was breathtaking, like a picture postcard. She seemed to intentionally avoid any discussion of her husband's troubles, talking instead about her vineyard and winery.

When they first moved to wine country, she told me, neither she nor her husband had any experience with farming grapes or making wine. She confessed that even her pallet for properly tasting and appreciating wine was woeful. She decided, early on, to gain as much knowledge about wine as she possibly could. This included several years of formal studies, eventually earning a certificate from the Court of Master Sommeliers.

"The Court of Master Sommeliers?" I asked. "What is that?"

"Oh, it's a bit like a degree in law, I suppose," she answered, "only designating an expertise in wine instead of law. A lot of studying and passing rather difficult exams to become certified."

"Kinda does sound a little like law school and the bar exam," I offered casually. I'd had no idea there was so much education involved in becoming a wine expert.

"Did you know that the Temecula Valley is the original California wine growing region?" she asked.

"I would have guessed Napa," I responded.

"Most people do not know this, but the very first vines to be planted for use as wine in all of California were planted right here by the monks of the San Juan Capistrano Mission. Most likely to be used for sacramental wine, I would imagine. But I'm sure the priests indulged in some imbibing on their own from time to time." She gave a dainty titter. "Then the area lay dormant for decades, because of prohibition and a variety of reasons. Until finally, in the 1960s, the Kaiser Land Development Company purchased an area known as Vail Ranch and began investing in and studying the Valley. Horticulturalists were brought in to evaluate what type of agricultural products could be grown. Along with avocados and oranges, the experts determined that vineyards were well suited for the valley. The cool moist air from the coast would settle in the Temecula Appellation in the evening and then burn off in the sun the following morning, perfect for grape growing."

"Gee, I had no idea. Pretty interesting," I commented genuinely.

At some point, Scatucci and Mr. Emsch joined us. Scatucci remarked about the view, just as I had. "On a clear day you can see all the way to the ocean," Mrs. Emsch informed him. To which Scatucci whistled appreciatively.

We four sat around the pool chatting like new friends, light-heartedly, rather than as lawyers with a client charged with serious crimes. Either Emsch was fearless, or Scatucci had assuaged his fears to a considerable extent with talk of prevailing in court. None of us on that pleasant afternoon in bucolic wine country could have possibly predicted the hell that would soon be unleashed just steps from where we now sat.

## CHAPTER SEVENTEEN

3 a.m. and Rose Emsch lay wide awake in bed staring into the darkness of the master bedroom, unable to sleep. The stress of her husband being arrested, police coming to their home, meeting with lawyers; it was all too much.

She wandered downstairs, pulled a dark bottle of Hendrick's off a shelf and made herself a gin & tonic, hoping it might make her sleepier. Walking outside to the patio, a thick blanket of Pacific Ocean fog had rolled in over the western hills as it often does, the vineyards soaking up the moisture till the sun rises to burn it away. Indeed, the very name Temecula allegedly means *where the sun shines through the mist*, translated from the native language of Luiseno Indians, the original inhabitants of the region. The gray dampness made her shiver.

Back inside, she saw the glow of her husband's computer screen atop his desk in the office. Both his and her laptops had been returned to them by the police. Seating herself at his desk, a few keystrokes and his recent search history was displayed.

"What the hell is all this?" she whispered to no one, reading the subject headers on the screen: Males as Slaves; Sexual Humiliation; Sexual Power Exchange; Forced Feminization; Dominatrix. Clicking the links, Rose sat mesmerized as images appeared, women wearing latex catsuits and stiletto heels dominating kneeling men groveling at their feet. Another click. A man wearing a frilly French maid costume cleaning a toilet while a woman brandishing a multi-tailed whip stood over him menacingly. Was this the sort of stuff that turned her husband on? She truly had no idea. She had always considered their sex life to be completely fulfilling. Why was he looking at such deviance online?

Clicking, scrolling, reading the online fetish sites, Rose lost track of time. It was all rather distressingly fascinating. She heard footsteps padding down the stairs. Looking up, she could see through the outside office window the sky beginning to take on a morning glow. Then, by the doorway stood her husband, sleepy-eyed and wearing pajamas.

"What are you doing up so early?" he asked.

"Sorry, I could not sleep," she replied, adding, "but I have had a most enlightening education visiting all the kinky sex sites on your computer." She watched his face turn crimson. "Any other secrets you would like to share with your wife?"

He felt violated. She had invaded his inner sanctum, his atelier, his man-cave. "Um, oh that stuff? That's nothing really. Just weird stuff I wandered across on the computer," he responded, trying to sound nonchalant.

"Eddy, this search history goes way back. It is not just stuff you accidentally wandered upon. Are you not satisfied with our love life?"

"Of course, I am," he replied, but seemingly at a loss for further explanation.

"No, really," Rose spoke with sincerity. "I need to know. Please. I'd like you to sit down and explain to me what all this means." She motioned for him to take a seat in a wingback chair across the room.

He sat, gingerly settling his body onto the chair.

"Clearly, I have embarrassed you. But I don't mean to. Sweetie, I am your wife. I want you to be completely honest with me."

He continued to sit in silence, not knowing what he could possibly say to her. In all the years they had been married, he had never revealed, never even hinted at, this side of himself. The situation he now suddenly found himself in terrified him.

She stood. "I'm going to the kitchen to make some coffee. When I return can we please talk about this? I mean, how long have you had these desires, these feelings?"

He watched her leave the room.

"It all began with A Man Called Horse," he said when she returned, reclaiming her seat at his desk.

"Excuse me?" she asked, perplexed. "What does a horse have to do with anything?"

"It's the title of a movie I saw when I was a kid. That's my earliest recollection of feeling this way."

"You'll need to explain that, I think," she said, giving a quizzical look.

"The movie was about this wealthy sophisticated English nobleman who was traveling through the old West with some other aristocrats. They were attacked by Indians. Sioux warriors, I believe. They killed all the other white men in the group but spared him because they were fascinated by his blond hair."

Rose cocked her head. "I'm not certain what blond hair has to do with anything, either. But please continue. I'm listening."

"So, the Indians brought him back to their camp where the chief gave him to one of the squaws to be her slave. The chief gave the squaw the Englishman as a sort of present. She put a rope around his neck and led him around like he was a horse, hence the title of the movie, I suppose. The women in the tribe mocked and humiliated him. He was forced to do chores for her, things considered women's work."

"Women's work?"

"Come on. You know. Domestic chores. Cooking, cleaning. Things the men in the tribe derogated as women's work."

Rose offered a dubious grunt, and he continued.

"Anyway, for some reason, it got me excited watching this cultured gentleman stripped of all his male pride and dominated by the squaws. Shit, I was just a kid at an impressionable age. You know, just discovering sex and all. Who the hell knows why that turned me on?"

"Eddy, Honey," his wife chuckled softly, "why have you never told me about these feelings of yours? I would have been more than happy to fire the housekeeper and let you do all the *women's work*."

"I'm baring my soul to you and you make a joke," he said, feigning hurt feelings while welcoming a bit of levity to mitigate his nervousness.

"I'm sorry," she replied. "Please continue. So, how have you satisfied these urges to be dominated by women? I know it's nothing we have ever engaged in."

"If you must know, professionals. I swear, I have never had sex with any of them. I just pay them to boss me around."

"To boss you around? You actually pay someone for this?"

"To mock and humiliate me. Like the Englishman in the movie," he explained, briefly considering whether to divulge that he enjoyed being faux-forced to dress in female clothing as part of his fantasy scene.

"Does this mean you are not satisfied with me?" she asked. "Because I really don't think I could do that. I've seen the photos of those dominatrix women on the internet sites you bookmarked. There's no way I see myself wearing those leather cat suits. I'd feel just plain silly. Plus, it's just not in me to treat you like that."

"No, no. Honey, I am completely happy with you and our sex life. It's perfect. What I'm talking about is not really sex ... it's hard to explain. It's just different. More mental. More like therapy than sex."

They continued talking for a long while. It was cathartic, a relief to finally share his deep longings with the woman he loved, experiencing a new level of trust that only seemed to elevate his esteem for this wonderful woman he'd married. And he told Rose about his relationship with the Chinese/Hawaiian mistress, including the way she tried to coerce him to kill her husband. A revelation that would ultimately become his undoing.

## CHAPTER EIGHTEEN

Rose began calling every number on her husband's phone that contained an 808 area code. The first dozen were all legitimate businesses and hotels. The thirteenth number was answered, but there was silence.

"Hello?" Rose spoke into the phone.

More silence.

"Hello," she repeated, "is anyone there?"

No one at the other end of the call spoke, but Rose could hear breathing.

"Ms. Cantu? We need to talk," Rose said.

The silence lingered.

"Ms. Cantu, my name is Rose Emsch. I believe you know my husband."

"Sissy?" came the splenetic response.

Rose felt instant revulsion upon hearing that single word, but quickly regained composure. "So, you *are* there. Good. Please listen then. My husband told me all about his ...uh, relationship ... with you."

"Did he now?"

"So, there is nothing you can say that I don't already know. Nothing to use as any sort of leverage against him."

Silence returned.

"Let me disabuse you of any notions to the contrary. Our life together was perfect as perfect can be, until he got involved with you. But I will not allow you to completely ruin our lives. So, listen carefully. So far, Eddy has told the police nothing of your intent to have your husband murdered. He has tried to distance himself from the entire incident. But if you have any further involvement with my husband, if you make any further allegations against him, try to drag him deeper into your sordid life and the unseemly situation regarding the missing man you claim to be your husband ... in fact, if I ever even hear your name uttered again, I will make certain the police know that it was you who tried to kill your husband. Eddy will testify that you specifically told him you wanted your husband dead and that you tried to blackmail him into helping you do it. Do you understand?"

A few indistinguishable words were all Rose heard from the other end. Speaking Chinese, Rose assumed.

"Leave us the hell alone!" Rose finally screamed into the phone before hanging up.

"What's with all the shouting?" Eddy asked, entering the room where his wife stood seething after terminating the call.

Rose told her husband about her threat to Cantu. Eddy stood transfixed.

"You spoke to her?"

Rose nodded.

"Oh, Rosie, you shouldn't have done that. Why couldn't you just stay out of it? Leave it alone?" He and Cantu had always communicated via email, but he committed her number to memory the day he accosted that accursed guy on his boat. For whatever reason, he then entered her number into his phone. A decision he now sorely regretted.

"The idea of that woman causing us so much trouble was just not something I could sit back idly and watch without doing something about it," she answered.

"Rose, you don't know this woman. Don't know the kind of person she is. She has video of me. Video that she threatened to post on the internet. The threat of exposing me online was what she used to try and get me to help her murder her husband."

"What sort of video?" Rose wanted to know. "I mean, how bad could it possibly be?"

"I'm not sure," he lied, knowing exactly what the video likely would show, "but I really would not want anyone to see it, whatever it may be." He knew there was a plethora of cross-dressers and drag queens who might not feel the least threatened by such a video, maybe they would even relish such exposure, but he was not among that ilk. Such a video would destroy him. Destroy his credibility in business and, he surmised, lead to the eventual ruination of his marriage.

"Eddy, I told her that I already know all about you and her. She no longer has any leverage against us. No reason for her to publish any sort of video."

"I hope you're right, honey," Eddy replied dubiously. "I really hope you are right."

## CHAPTER NINETEEN

# BEN HARDING

Sammie and I were sitting on the front deck of my house, glasses of vino in our hands, watching as sailboats dotting the horizon chased puffs of wind, the setting sun turning the sky a brilliant orange.

"So beautiful," she said. "So very perfect. You are really lucky to live here and enjoy this view every evening."

"You're right," I agreed. "Only one thing would make it more perfect."

"Hm?" she responded absently, still watching the setting sun.

"You," I told her. "If you were here every evening enjoying it with me."

Raising her glass to her lips, she sipped, still staring out toward the ocean.

"Samantha, you know I've been in love with you since practically forever. These past months spending time together again has been wonderful."

"Wonderful?" she repeated, questioning.

"Sure. It got off to a bit of a rocky start. What with the

disappearance of Gavin and all. But you know I'm always here for you. And I kinda feel that his disappearance, tragic as it may be, has brought us together and, in a weird way, something good came of it."

"I think I know what you mean, all of it and none of it. I don't even understand what I just said, and yet I do," Sammie equivocated, casting her gaze downward as if examining something at her feet. "But I do know that being with you again has made me realize how very much you mean to me, Ben. Absolutely."

"So, move in with me," I offered. "Live with me here at the beach. Hell, marry me. Let's enjoy sunsets together forever."

She smiled. "Well, it certainly would be a lot more convenient than all this commuting back and forth between my house in the valley and here. I swear, I must have put a ton of miles on my car these last few months. It's leased. They charge me up the wazoo if I exceed the allotted mileage."

"Then do it," I pushed. "Move in with me. *Me casa es su casa.*"

She touched my cheek with her hand. "Oh Ben, I do not deserve you." I wasn't certain if her tone was sincere or merely patronizing, till she added, "But we really are good together, aren't we?"

"You bet we are," I answered with enthusiasm. "You could rent out your house easy. Or sell it! You could make a huge profit. Live here. No mortgage on this place."

"Oh, so romantically stated," she laughed.

"Well, I know you are a very practical lady, so just pointing out the facts. If not for love, then for convenience. I'll take it any way I can get it."

"Hmmm, well, okay, I will ..."

"You will?" I interrupted.

"I was going to say, I will ... consider it."

"Procrastination?"

"I'm not a procrastinator. I just like to put some things off until later."

Her logic caused me to smile.

"No, I mean it. I will seriously consider your gracious proposal. Absolutely."

Time seemed to momentarily stop as her answer sunk in. I could hear the waves crashing loudly onto the shore. The sun had now fully set. The sky suddenly brilliant with stars. She leaned closer and kissed me, tracing her hand along my thigh. "You said you'd take it any way you can get it. So, take it, take me, right now." She stood up and walked inside the house, leading me along like a tethered pet.

Inside the bedroom, unbuttoning her sundress and letting it fall to the floor. She stood for but a brief moment silhouetted in the dim light before slipping gracefully onto the bed and under the sheets. I stood watching her for a long moment before undressing and joining her.

"You know something?" she quietly whispered, snuggling close. "I've been in love with you since practically forever, too."

# CHAPTER TWENTY

The call came from an 808 area code. "Hello?" Samantha said, grabbing the ringing cell phone from atop a stack of clothing she was sorting from her closet in anticipation of potentially moving to the beach. But she was met only with silence. "Hello!" she said again, with agitation.

"Oh, yes, Samantha. Samantha Zimmah?"

Sammie knew immediately who it was. "Hello Connie," she said, sidestepping shoes and items scattered about the floor. "Why are you calling?"

"Samantha, I am wondering if you could perhaps help me," Connie Cantu began.

"With what?" She never liked this woman and was getting annoyed just hearing her voice on the phone.

"Samantha? I am very much desperate or I would not be bothering you. You see, since Gavin disappeared, I have no money. No income. Nobody to support me."

"My, how awful," came Samantha's reply, dripping with sarcasm.

"All the bank money is frozen," her voice a bleating noise. "The banks will give me no money because my name not on accounts. I tell them, community property. Gavin's money is automatically half mine. But they not listen at all."

Racing through a dozen mental calisthenics to keep herself from saying something she might regret, Samantha responded. "Perhaps that's because Gavin's money is *not* half yours. The way I understand it, as it was explained to me by my darling lawyer Ben, inherited money is *not* community property. Gavin inherited his fortune from his brother, Griffin, when he died. So, even though you might have tricked Gavin into marrying you, it is not automatically yours. Surely you remember Griffin? You know, the brother you were involved with while he was still married to me? The brother you had somehow wrapped around your little finger until he was murdered? The brother whose estate you tried to steal from me, his lawful wife? The brother who I still feel you had a role in his death? And then you moved onto Gavin?"

"Yes, of course I remember bruddah. Very, very unfortunate. But I did not never trick anybody. Griffin was good man. Griffin would not want me to suffer or be poor. And neither would Gavin. Samantha, this is all such a mess."

"Yes, I'm sure it is," Sammie replied.

"Soon, very soon, I will be evicted from the marina where our boat is. I have not been paying the slip rent. What can I do? I would sell boat, but title in Gavin's name not mine," her weak wavering cry continued.

"I see," Sammie replied, devoid of compassion for this querulous woman.

"I really thought I would have money from insurance company by now. But they say, no can pay because Gavin's body not found. They cannot be certain he is truly dead without body. But I know he is truly dead."

"Um hm, and how is it that *you* know?"

"I know because I can feel it. I can feel that his presence is no longer with us here in the world of the living."

"I see."

"Samantha, all I ask is enough money to live until insurance pays death benefit to me as Gavin's spouse. Just a loan, that is all. I will repay when insurance money comes."

Sammie rolled her eyes. "That could be years. No, I'm sorry, but I can't help you."

"You cannot or you won't?" Cantu snapped.

Feeling a mean thrill shoot through her from Cantu's situation, some *schadenfreude* as her mother used to say, Sammie snapped back with vituperation. "You know what? I am not at all sorry. I cannot, and will not, help you. You are such bad news. No good ever seems to come to people who associate with you. So, go fuck yourself! Do not call me again ... unless Gavin is found. And, even then, have *him* call me, not you!"

CHAPTER TWENTY-ONE

Rose found her husband hunched over his desk, his head in his hands. "What's wrong?" she asked.

"I hope I'm not making a mistake. I've agreed to testify against the Cantu woman. The police somehow found email correspondence between us, and my testimony will connect the dots that what she was asking was for me to murder her husband."

"So, what's the problem," Rose wanted to know.

"Well, my story is that she solicited me to kill her husband, but I turned her down. And, based upon my testimony coupled with the emails, they are going with the idea that she, then, found someone else to do her dirty work."

"Works for me," Rose said. "That is most likely the exact the way it happened."

"Unless the whole thing somehow turns around and bites me on the ass. What if the police change their theory and decide I was complicit?"

"That won't happen," Rose assured.

Leaning back in his chair, looking out the window toward the expansive lawn beyond, then turning his gaze upon his wife, said, "I think maybe you should go back up to L.A., visit your sister for a few days. I need some time alone to sort all this shit out, to deal with it all."

"How are you going to deal with it? Let me help you."

"No, really. I hate it that you are involved in all this mess. Let me figure out how best to deal with it. Please, I'm asking you, go visit your sister for a while."

## CHAPTER TWENTY-TWO

They were speaking Spanish. That is what grabbed Connie Cantu's attention. Right there on the dock, across from her boat, two dark-haired men looking in her boat's direction, speaking Spanish. Not something you hear every day at Ala Wai Yacht Harbor. Japanese, pidgin, German, Chinese, even French perhaps, and of course English but, for whatever reason, very seldom Spanish.

She emerged from the cabin below onto the aft deck carrying a steaming cup of saimin. They were walking over toward her boat. In the marina where boat people generally looked like boat people they seemed a *lubberly lot*, as her husband might say. Both men dressed in dark business suits, but they did not look like cops. One substantially taller than the other and wearing a red necktie, the shorter one tieless with a mustache. The red tie man waved at her. She briefly considered disappearing below deck again but decided to stay put, see what these two were up to.

"May we have a word with you, Mrs. Gambil?" the one with the red tie asked in perfect English, but with a hint of accent.

"What about?" she responded. "You're not police."

"Just a few moments of your time, please," the red tie answered politely, as they began to board the yacht without being invited.

"Gee, that smells delicious," the shorter one remarked, sniffing the aroma from her cup. "What is it, if I may ask?" His mustache, a lacquered filigree of fuzz beneath his nose, bobbed up and down as he spoke.

"Saimin," Cantu answered, not offering any.

"I've never heard of that," he said.

"My, how surprising," came her sarcastic reply.

He just stood there, smiling at her.

"It's soup. The name saimin comes from two Chinese words meaning thin and noodle. It is a dashi soup with soft egg noodles, green onions, kamaboko, cha siu, and sliced Spam."

"Seriously? Spam?" the red tie said with a slight laugh. "That doesn't sound very Chinese."

"What? You some kinda expert on Asian food?" Cantu snapped. "It not Chinese but Spam is in nearly everything here in Hawaii."

"Spam?" the taller one repeated, shaking his head. "Never would have guessed."

"If you never tried," Cantu said, still not offering any, "then you just don't know."

A few more minutes of small talk followed, with admiring comments about her yacht and the beauty of Honolulu.

"Yes, yes, thank you very much," Connie finally cut them off. "I'm sure you did not come here just to talk about Spam and admire my boat. Who are you and what is the real reason why you are here?"

The men's faces shifted instantly from friendly to stern. "You don't get to ask the questions, we do. Better you do not know who sent us or who we are," the taller man told her.

"Tell us about your relationship with Mr. Eddy Emsch," the mustached shorter one demanded with a menacing tone.

"What relationship?" Cantu replied.

"Please, don't be cute. Just tell us what you know about Emsch," the mustache waving up and down at her as he spoke.

Cantu stared into the eyes of the men, considering her response. "We were having an affair. He fell in love, but I am a married woman, so I broke it off."

"Look, Mrs. Gambil ... or perhaps you prefer being called Mistress Cantu?" the taller man said aggressively, moving close enough to encroach upon her personal space. "You need to tell us everything you know, and I mean everything, about Emsch. Be a shame to see this beautiful boat sink right here in the marina. Maybe even with its owner still aboard."

She tried dancing around the subject, the two men quickly making it quite clear they had no tolerance for any games. They asked if Emsch ever discussed his mainland business with her? Did he ever talk about being involved with drugs or name anyone he does business with? The two men grew increasingly threatening with each question.

"Ever hear the name Rojas Raton?" one of them asked.

She had not. But, she decided, if these two were so hell-bent on getting information about Edward Emsch, it appeared clearly in her best interests to *lawe kapakahi*, provide whatever she knew. So, with no further pretext, she told them the tidbits of his drug connections, the stuff that Emsch would often share with her as a way of impressing her. And she told them about the arrangement she had with Sissy, about his fetish for humiliation, forced cross-dressing and female dominance. At first the men appeared not to believe this part. They began to get ever more aggressive, pushing her toward the edge of the yacht. She feared they might shove her overboard.

"I have proof!" she snapped, slithering away from them, retreating below, and returning with laptop in hand. "I videoed some of our sessions together."

The two men looked at each other in disbelief. "He let you tape him?"

"I used a hidden camera. Mistah Emsch did not know he was being filmed."

"Okay, you've piqued my interest. Let's see what you got."

Opening her laptop, she played a video of Sissy prancing daintily around the room, petticoat billowing with each pseudo girlish twirl, then on his knees, crawling on all fours to the regally seated Mistress Cantu and kissing her stiletto-clad feet.

The men burst into laughter and began speaking to each other in rapid Spanish. Then, in English, "We are going to need a copy of that video, Mrs. Gambil."

CHAPTER TWENTY-THREE

# BEN HARDING

Just another perfect California day. Riding bicycles along the beach bike path with Sammie, we pause for a moment to take in the splendor of the sun shimmering off the blue Pacific. There is a lone swimmer out there and he is accompanied by several dolphins leaping alongside him as he breaststrokes through the water. Out in the distance Santa Catalina Island is clearly visible, *twenty-six miles across the sea,* as the old song goes, but looking so close as if the swimmer could simply swim there. Samantha and I stand inches apart, straddling our bikes, holding hands and sharing the sight. Can life get any better than this? The only way it could is for this woman at my side to share every day like this with me. We have discussed moving in together, but she has not committed yet. She says she is "considering" the idea. As for me, forget mere cohabitation; I would marry her in a heartbeat.

Maybe I should feel guilty for feeling so happy. I mean, it was a series of very unfortunate circumstances that brought us together. A lot of bad stuff. First her husband dies. Murdered, as it turned out. Then someone she cares a great deal about, her brother-in-law, goes missing. Presumably dead. Perhaps murdered as well. Do I have any right to feel so giddy in the face of so many calamitous events? Probably not, but I cannot help it. Being reunited with Samantha Zimmer was the best thing to ever happen to me. No matter the circumstances.

We resume peddling our bikes, leaving the swimmer and dolphins behind. Riding side by side for the better part of a mile, then Sammie suddenly peddles faster, pulling out in front as if challenging me to a race. I let her maintain the lead for several minutes, lagging behind, admiring the shape of her derriere and the way the wind is blowing her hair. From any angle, she is worth admiring. Then, peddling with a vengeance, I overtake her. She pours it on and catches up again. Another mile and we slow way down, out of breath, laughing, perspiration glistening on our foreheads. It's a great day. I'll take all of these I can get.

Late afternoon, we pop over to the Baskin-Robbins on Washington Boulevard near the Venice Pier for some ice cream. Sitting at one of the brightly colored round tables enjoying our treats, I look over to see Scatucci at the counter placing an order. "Dude!" I shout to get his attention.

He looks up absently, confused, as if in a brain fog and trying to recall just who I am. Then recognition sets in, accompanied by his trademark smiling greeting, "*Paesan*! Sorry, my brain was elsewhere."

He appears a few pounds heavier than last time I saw him. I comment on it, jovially.

"Fuck, I know, right? I've been doing nothing but working lately. Got a big trial coming up. Just sitting for hours, analyzing files, strategizing. I eat, I drink, I work. Finally decided I needed an ice cream break, so here I am. But have not gotten any exercise in weeks. "

"What else aren't you getting?" Sammie joked, remembering the waitress from Baja Cantina and the womanizing reputation of which Ben had informed her. The man clearly suffered from some sort of sexual addiction, Sammie was convinced.

"Ah, well there are certain things a man just cannot go too long without," he joked back. Then leaning closer to me, placing a conspiratorial hand near his mouth as if conveying something confidential he did not want Samantha to hear, "One of the perks about the Bella case? All I gotta do is call her up and within an hour there's a gorgeous female knocking on my door. No pre-merger negotiation necessary, just bang and done, quick and easy. No charge. She knows it takes the edge off so I can concentrate better on her case." He laughs.

But Samantha hears the comment, grimly shaking her head in phony sympathy. "I am so glad I'm not a man," she says curtly. "I prefer to do all my thinking with just one head."

"It's a curse. It really is," Scatucci's blithe riposte. "Well, gotta bolt. Too much time away from the case tends to make my legal brain shut down." He grabs a bag containing a pint of freshly scooped peanut butter chocolate ice cream and heads for the door. "Ciao."

# CHAPTER TWENTY-FOUR

Rojas Raton was appalled. The video on his screen showed the man he had been doing business with doing some very odd things. Despicable things that totally disgusted Raton. The figure on the screen was dressed like some macabre little girl, crawling on hands and knees, kissing the feet of some short little Asian woman. The men had presented the video to their boss thinking it outrageously humorous and to be used, perhaps, as blackmail. But Rojas found nothing amusing about what he was watching.

Raton shook his head, bewildered. Such a tiny woman and such a large man. Raton did not understand what he was seeing or why the man, Mr. Emsch, would be subjecting himself to her like that. He knew such weirdos existed but would never have taken Emsch for such *bicho raro*. Raton felt outrage that this was someone with whom he had been doing business. "*Pervertido!*" He spat the word like an obscenity. "This is not a man!" he declared. "Where are his *cojones*? He does not deserve to continue in this world as a man. And the woman? *La puta. Asquerosa. Madre de Dios, lo siento,* I have no words for such a woman."

## CHAPTER TWENTY-FIVE

# BEN HARDING

Samantha was relaxing on the living room sofa watching television and I was in the kitchen preparing dinner for us, my famous Malibu-chicken-pierogi, when I heard her shout, "Ben, come in here. Scatucci is on TV."

I rushed into the room, standing behind the sofa where Sammie was sitting, and watched as a local news reporter was speaking to her audience from outside a courthouse. "…Claire Annette Michaelson, also known as Bambini Bella, has had all charges dismissed for allegedly operating a high-priced international prostitution ring that catered to celebrities, politicians and wealthy professionals. Michaelson, thirty-nine years of age, was being held in Los Angeles County Jail after the judge refused to allow Michaelson's release on bail, holding that she represented a flight risk. But now a Van Nuys Superior Court jury has acquitted her on three counts of felony pimping, with the court dismissing all further charges, including drug charges." As the reporter was talking, a video was being shown of Bambini Bella entering the courtroom earlier in the day with her attorney, Vincent Scatucci. Not looking at all like some downtrodden person who had been spending time in jail, she strode into the room looking poised and confident, wearing a short black knit sweater dress and thigh-high black boots, her hair pulled back in a clip.

The video ended. Scatucci could now be seen *live* emerging onto the stairs outside the courthouse with the reporter rushing to interview him. "Mr. Scatucci, do you have any comment regarding your client's criminal acquittal today?"

Scatucci calmly answered. "Well, of course I am pleased with today's events. And it should be noted that this was an alleged crime without any victims here. The only victim is my client. Her reputation has been severely tarnished by these proceedings. This is not a bad person, as the press has portrayed her. She is a person who committed no crime that she has been convicted of and was subjected to senseless public humiliation beyond the pale. There is no one who could say, 'She hurt me' or 'My life is worse because of her.' There was no evidence of violence, drug use, squandered money, theft, or any other conduct that would create a victim. I might point out that at the hearing Deputy District Attorney Ellington even admitted that my client's prior criminal history contained only minor offenses. And the judge even thought that the charges brought against her were excessive. In the end, the DA grossly overreached, and this can only be viewed as a clear victory for the defense."

"Can you tell us, what was your client's reaction, her state of mind, to today's acquittal and dismissal?"

"She had no drastic reaction, though she is pleased with the outcome. Her state of mind is only that this proceeding was grossly unfair."

"The judge in this matter stated he denied bail not only because she may be a flight risk, but also called your client an unremorseful and pathetic person. Do you have any comment on that?"

"I certainly think such comments are out of line for a sitting judge," Scatucci replied. "And I completely disagree with that characterization. Those descriptions were unfounded personal opinions that he should keep to himself if he wears the robes."

"Mr. Scatucci, during the trial several women allegedly employed by your client testified that they had sex with the men that your client provided and that they gave your client forty percent of what they were paid. Can you confirm that to be true?"

"I'm not going to comment on that," he answered.

The reporter pressed further. "Also, a so-called *trick book* introduced into evidence detailed several prostitute names, prostitution appointments, money received, and clients' names. Are you able to tell us anything about the clients listed in the book?"

"Well, you are correct that there was such a book introduced but I did not recognize most of those names, though a few were prominent in politics and entertainment."

"The book also supposedly contained information concerning an alleged affair she personally had with a Beverly Hills police detective who was investigating her escort business. And during her testimony she contended the relationship played a crucial role in shielding her from prosecution during an earlier investigation. Care to make any comment on that?"

"I know nothing of any so-called affair with any of the Beverly Hills law enforcement. Although a Rolodex and log of her alleged customers has been marked as evidence in the case, and many of the names contained therein had been blacked out. The police claim they blacked out the names in court records to protect innocent individuals. That's really all I can say."

"Thank you so much, Mr. Scatucci." Vinnie hastily walked

away as the reporter signed off. "That was Vincent G. Scatucci, attorney for Claire Annette Michaelson, better known as Bambini Bella. Reporting live from the Van Nuys courthouse, this is Amanda Lynn. Now back to you in the studio."

"Gotta say," I spoke to the back of Samatha's head as she remained seated on the sofa with me standing behind, "my buddy, the redoubtable Vinnie Scatucci, was looking damn good. He answered that reporter's questions with all the smoothness of a 1940s crooner."

"A crooner, sure," Sammie replied with raised eyebrows. "Interesting metaphor. The whole thing sounded kinda musical to me. The reporter's name is Amanda Lynn – as in, a mandolin, get it? And Vinnie's client? Claire Annette – a clarinet. Even her fake name is musical: Bella. Now there's a real *ringer*."

Ben was cracking up. This is what being in love must feel like, two grown people sharing childishly silly jokes. "Kiddo," he told her, "That's one of the million reasons why I love you. We both have the same goofy sense of humor. By the way, when Vinnie first told me his client's real name, I had the very same thought."

## CHAPTER TWENTY-SIX

It was four o'clock in the morning when the call was placed to Vincent Scatucci that started him on another two-and-a-half-hour drive from L.A. to Temecula. The elaborate Paniolo Rose gates at the bottom of the long driveway were open, but a squad car and four armed police blocked access when Scatucci arrived. Vincent identified himself and was allowed to drive his Beamer up the hill to the main house, the sun rising at an angle in the sky making the windows seem ablaze, shining in his eyes, making it difficult to see. He parked next to a fountain located in the center of the circular drive. The place was abuzz with police activity.

Making his way through the residence, out to the rear yard, near the cabana and swimming pool, then down a steep hill and along a gravel path leading to the winery tasting room where a large group of law enforcement personnel gathered. As Scatucci approached, peering over the shoulders of several uniforms, he saw a video on continuous loop being played on a computer atop an outdoor table. It appeared to be a man dressed like Minnie Pearl sans the hat, dancing, then crawling across a tile floor toward a bantam-looking female half his size wearing black leather, who was seated nearby passively watching. Scatucci looked closer. The man was Eddy Emsch.

"What the hell?" Scatucci muttered.

"You the lawyer?" he heard a plainclothes officer ask from behind.

Scatucci swung around to face the officer. "Yes. Vincent G. Scatucci, attorney for Edward Emsch."

"Sorry counselor, your client's dead."

"What? How?" Scatucci asked, trying to curb his alarm.

"Found him hanged. Dangling from an open beam in the ceiling at the far end of the tasting room."

"And the video I just watched?"

"Posted on the internet. Don't know by who, but it sure as hell wasn't posted by your client. So far, five thousand views. It was playing when we arrived."

"Jesus," the lawyer muttered. "Looks like he was into some pretty kinky shit. And the poor bastard killed himself over it?"

"He was dressed in that same get-up when the body was discovered," the officer added. "Died in drag."

"Hung himself, you say?"

"Well, one might initially assume that was the case. One thing, though. It was not a suicide."

"How so?" Scatucci wondered aloud.

"Hmm. Well, for starters, the blood. Lots of blood. Puce colored. That whole foofy dress he was dolled up in, and female undergarments, everything stained with blood. Pools of blood on the floor under him, too."

"Blood from what?" Scatucci asked.

"Caponized," the officer answered.

The lawyer gave a look of not understanding.

"Severed genitals," the officer restated, matter-of-factly.

"His dick was cut off?"

"Testicles too. And they are missing," the officer answered.

"Also, severed tongue. The tongue was found by his crotch, stuffed inside the panties, where his dick used to be."

"What the fuck?" Scatucci uttered, incredulous.

"I know," the officer replied. "Can't tell yet whether cause of death was from hanging or blood loss. Either way, must've been a horrifying and painful way to go. In my twenty-five years on the job, this has gotta be the weirdest, sickest thing I've ever come across."

"I usta be a cop too," Scatucci told the officer. "In Detroit. Tough town, but never saw anything like this before, either."

Unfortunately, Scatucci *had* actually seen similarly gruesome scenes during his days with the FBI and DEA. What agents called a Colombian necktie. A form of execution where the victim's tongue is pulled through a deep cut beneath the jaw and left dangling on the neck. A method of psychological warfare designed to scare and intimidate. Other variations might be stuffing the genitals of dead men into their mouths; or killing a pregnant woman, extracting the fetus, and replacing it with a rooster or a pig. All meant to send a message and to dehumanize. What he was looking at certainly seemed to fit that method of degradation, though Scatucci was keeping such speculation to himself. He had hoped never to encounter such scenes again, it was the reason he quit being any sort of policeman and went to law school.

"Yep, pretty fucked up," the cop agreed, soberly nodding his head. "What can you tell me about the wife?"

"Mrs. Emsch? I only met her one time. Seems like a real nice lady. Classy. You thinkin' she's somehow involved in this?" Scatucci sounded skeptical.

"Can't say. A couple female officers are with her right now. She's being questioned," the cop told him. "It was the wife who asked for you to be called. Not lawyering up, she just wanted you to know what's going on."

"Yeah, I don't do homicide. Just handle drug cases. And prostitution. Defend the rights of those accused, but I draw the line at murder cases."

"I see," the officer responded with an icy air of disdain and seemingly no further interest in talking with a turncoat cop. A cop turned criminal defense lawyer was the lowest of the low in his book. Starting to walk away, hurling over his shoulder a contemptuous parting remark, "So, you used to be in law enforcement, but now you defend criminals. Drug pushing whores and pimps, just not murderers. A man's gotta draw the line somewhere, I suppose."

Connie Cantu-Gambil was tapped out. People talk about having out-of-body experiences but I'm having an out-of-money experience, she thought to herself with sardonic resolve. Every day she found notices attached to her boat or her dock box warning of legal action if the slip rent was not paid immediately. Immediately was too soon. No way she could raise the amount due that had piled up over so many months. Water and electricity were provided by the marina, but they were threatening to disrupt service, and even to tow her yacht away. She had never established any form of credit in her own name. And, in her entire adult life, there were only two tangible assets of monetary value she had ever owned outright. There was the California house her husband's deceased brother purchased for her – that she had sold years ago, the money long-since spent to pay for lawyers in her fight trying to validate her claim in Griffin's will, and defense lawyers regarding early threatened criminal allegations surrounding Griffin's untimely death, as well as using a large chunk of the proceeds to support herself before marrying Gavin. The only remaining asset being the Mercedes Benz that same foolish man had gifted her. Selling her Mercedes might buy her some time, but then how would she get around?

She was running out of options. With her husband passed and his bank accounts frozen, her only source of income was from slaves paying for her services, but times were lean. That barely brought in enough money for food and basic necessities. *Where the hell are all the damn perverts when I need them?* She had even swallowed what little remaining pride she had and called the mainland but her pleading for help from Samantha Zimmer had fallen on deaf ears. *That haole bitch!*

# CHAPTER TWENTY-EIGHT

It was pouring rain when Vincent Scatucci arrived at the jail and parked in a designated parking area. His first step out of the car sloshed into a pothole of water, soaking the left shoe of a six-hundred-dollar pair of black lizard-skin loafers. "Shit," he muttered. He shuffled into the building through the security check point, a wet swishing noise with each step of his sopping left shoe, walked to a long desk staffed by a single uniformed officer, produced his California Bar card, and spoke the name of the inmate he was there to see.

An armed officer escorted him to a small beige-colored room with a single chair facing a thick wall of glass. A telephone hung near the glass. Soon a man dressed in an orange jump suit appeared on the other side, sat down, and picked up the phone located on his side of the glass.

"Thank you for contacting me," Scatucci spoke into his phone. "What can I do for you, Mr. Raton?"

"I'll tell ya what you can do for me," the prisoner answered. "You can get me the fuck outa here, for starters."

"I'm familiar with your case ...," Scatucci began.

"I already know you are familiar with my case. You were representing the guy I'm accused of doing business with. The winemaker, Mr. Emsch. A man who I recently discovered was not really much of a man at all. So, let us not beat around the mulberry bush, Mr. Scatucci. From what I am told, when it comes to handling drug cases, you come highly recommended. I find it quite admirable that you are able to use your former FBI and DEA experience as a tool against the police. I can really respect that. I watched with interest on the television evening news the way you got that madam off. Bambini Bella, love that name. I was greatly impressed with how you managed to get all drug charges dismissed along with the other more publicized charges. And those redacted names in her trick book. I'm sure you used that as leverage. A Beverly Hills detective having an affair with the accused, now that was amusing. And cleverly covered up. Very skillful, Mr. Scatucci. A win-win for everybody: the high-profile customers in that book were shielded, the detective never identified, and charges were dropped. That's what I want, a win-win for me. And I know there is no ... what do they call it? *Conflict of interest* with your other client, because Emsch is outa the picture, isn't he?"

"How do you know about Mr. Emsch no longer being my client?" Scatucci asked. There had been virtually no media coverage of the horrific events in Temecula. The police had kept a tight lid on it up to now.

"Good news just travels fast," Raton replied smugly. "The guy was a prick. Oh, wait a minute. I guess the word prick no longer *attaches* to him, does it?" He leaned back and laughed so hard he nearly fell out of the small metal chair on which he was seated.

"Am I to infer that you had something to do with that?" Scatucci inquired.

"Abso-fucking-lutely ... NOT. I am a completely innocent man."

"So, it's just some sort of weird coincidence that the man who was my client and most likely to implicate you is now dead? And you happen to know a fact about Emsch's death, the genital mutilation, that wasn't reported in the media?"

Rojas shrugged his shoulders, as if to indicate he had no answer, then offered, "Coincidences often involve a lot of planning, don't you think, Mr. Scatucci?"

This was already smelling bad to Vincent. "I do not handle murder cases," Scatucci informed him.

"I'm not hiring you to represent me in a murder case. I'm not accused of any murder. And I already told you, I'm one totally innocent hombre. I would never so much as harm a fly."

They began discussing the drug charges. At some point, the matter of a retainer arose, for legal fees. The Sixth Amendment includes the right to hire a lawyer of the defendant's choosing, at least as long as the person has the money to pay for it. But an accused's ill-gotten assets can be frozen until the criminal case is completed, often preventing them from obtaining representation by high-priced defense lawyers, thereby being relegated to public defenders. Scatucci was well aware that drug dealers often have difficulty producing funds that can be shown to be the product of a legitimate business venture, untainted by illegal narcotics trades.

"Feds confiscated all my money, but don't worry, you'll get paid," Rojas assured Scatucci. "I got small piles of *dinero* stashed away here and there for rainy days. Looks to me like it might start raining any day now."

"By law I cannot accept dirty money," Scatucci protested. "Any money illegally obtained is dirty, whether it's confiscated or not."

"Don't play cute with me. We already know you are fully capable of bending all sorts of rules to obtain a victory. Besides, as far as you're concerned, this ain't dirty money. It's legitimate cash I squirreled away over the years for emergencies. Totally clean, totally legit. So don't go worrying your pretty little head about it. All you gotta do is take a little side trip to get it, that's all." Rojas Raton had $250,000 of untraceable funds buried in a wall and offered it as retainer. However, the wall was located inside a condo in Naples.

"That's a pretty decent retainer. As long as you assure me it's not dirty, I guess I could make a trip down to Florida," Scatucci agreed, vaguely nodding his head.

Raton gave another huge chortle. "Wouldn't that be nice? Wouldn't that be easy? Sorry, counselor, no. I don't keep that sort of loose dinero in the States. It's in Napoli, Italia," Raton responded, using a mock Italian accent and waving his hands as he spoke about the location.

Scatucci gave an unnerving sigh.

"Oh, come on, Mr. Lawyer. Money is money. So what if you need to take a little jaunt over the pond to Italy? You're Italian, right? Go visit the homeland. Drink some vino, eat some pasta. Make it a vacation. Fuck, bill me for all your goddamned travel time. I don't give a shit. Just go get your money, then get me outa here. Understand?"

Jail is a short-time version of prison with the same dehumanization methods employed for volume control, the same lack of access to the world outside the walls of the institution, the same absence of the basic dignities of human existence. In his role as an attorney, Vincent Scatucci had visited the insides of many detention facilities. He was always anxious to be leaving after his business was done, leaving the strange scariness of such places and the prisoners within behind. This time, though, he felt as if he were carrying the foul fetor and malignant character of the place out with him.

To take on Raton as a client was a dubious decision. And fetching potentially illegal funds from a foreign nation might prove to be a tricky operation. An impromptu trip to Italy and carrying around a quarter mil in cash sounded just a tad too risky an undertaking for an officer of the court, such as himself, to personally carry out. The next day, Scatucci called his law clerk into his office. "Rivlen, how'd you like a little vacay to Italy?"

## CHAPTER TWENTY-NINE

# BEN HARDING

It happened at lunch. That's when the pieces finally came together. I was chowing down with Vinnie Scatucci at a little Mexican joint just off the Venice Pier called El Tarasco. Plowing into my usual, an all-beef burrito supreme topped with melted cheese and sour cream, while Scatucci regaled me with a crazy tale about how one of his clients died.

"So, there was this video looping on the internet, starring my client. In drag, dressed like Little Bo Peep, crawling around on all fours, kissing the feet of some chick who had her back to the camera. It was playing on a laptop near where they found his body."

"So, how'd he die?" I asked.

"He was hanged," Scatucci said, dipping a tortilla chip into a small bowl of salsa.

"Suicide?"

"That's what I thought at first, but nope. Not only was this guy still dressed like Little Bo Peep when they found him, but his dick was cut off. Balls too. Nobody commits suicide like that," he said definitively. "Nobody."

"Jesus! I'm trying to eat," I said, cramming a large piece of gooey tortilla down my maw.

"Yeah, sorry. If you would'a been there to see all the blood and stuff, you wouldn't be able to eat for a month." He laughed. "Might do ya some good, though. Lose some of that belly you're packin'."

I gave him an indignant look.

"Just kidding, *paesano*. You look in great shape. Not me. I can't seem to lose these five pounds I picked up over the winter."

"Five?" I questioned.

"Okay, ten pounds. Asshole," he answered, a string of melted cheese clinging to his chin that he wiped away with a paper napkin.

"Your client sounds pretty messed up psychologically," I said. "How can you be so sure it wasn't suicide? Maybe he had some sort of love/hate thing going on with his penis and decided to clip it off as he hanged himself."

"Nice theory, except the penis was missing. Nowhere to be found," Scatucci explained.

"Jesus," was all I could utter. "So, it was definitely murder then?"

"Gotta be. But, ready for this? So, the guy's wife comes to my office just the other day. Gorgeous broad. Dressed to the nines. Beautiful face. Great legs, great tits, the whole package. Nice lady, too." He stopped to take a bite from his taco, then went on with garbled words as he chewed the food. "Says she knows who killed her husband."

"Did she tell you who?" I asked, scooping up melted cheese from my plate with a chip.

"Says he was murdered because he was about to testify in a murder investigation. Says it was to shut him up. Murdered by a woman. Apparently, first she tried to blackmail him with the video. Threatened to post it on the internet unless he agreed not to testify. When that didn't work, she murdered him. Or had him murdered."

"Good grief. That's intense, man," I commented.

Scatucci waved his hand, dismissively. "I'm not really sure how much of what she told me is actually credible." The look on his face indicated he had reason to doubt the woman's story, or at least part of it.

"But did she give you a name? Did she say who it was that did the deed?" I asked, between bites.

"She said it was some hooker."

"A hooker?"

"Yeah. I was just representing my guy on some massive drug charges, was not fully up to speed on this other stuff. But supposedly the hooker was married to some guy and arranged to have him whacked. Apparently, my client was a customer of hers and somehow found out about her plan to kill her husband. That's what he was going to testify about."

"This hooker have a name?"

"Said it was some Chinese chick all the way over in Hawaii named Cantu."

I started to choke on the salsa in my mouth. Scatucci had to actually slap me on the back to stop the choking. "Are you fucking kidding me?" I stammered when able to speak.

"No, why?"

"A Chinese woman in Hawaii named Cantu? Gotta be the same woman," I said.

"What same woman?" Scatucci had no clue.

So, I told Vinnie all about Connie Cantu and how she was married to Gavin, Sammie's ex-husband's brother, and that Gavin had gone missing. Presumed dead.

"Fuck, that's incredible, *paesan*," he replied. "Hey, is this the missing person Samantha was telling me about the evening we met at Baja Cantina?"

"Yes. I forgot about that, but yes."

Scatucci sat chewing his food, staring out the window at traffic moving in all directions along Washington Boulevard.

"So, who is this client and his wife we're talking about?" I asked at last.

Taking a sip from his beverage to wash it down, he answered, "Emsch. The hubby/wife wine folks. You met them."

I drove out to Samantha's house in the Valley to tell her what I had discovered. It was the least I could do. Connie Cantu, who Sammie had always felt certain was involved in her husband's murder, and now Gavin's disappearance, was the same woman believed to be involved in Eddy Emsch's murder as well. Samantha became overwrought, demanding that we drive out to Temecula immediately to speak with Mrs. Emsch. I'd been there before and knew the way.

Rose Emsch remembered me from my previous visit with Scatucci. Her demeanor tenebrous and remarkably calm as she sat down with Sammie and me on the same patio overlooking the vineyards as before. Almost like she had maybe taken a sedative. We three sat in silence for several very long uncomfortable moments before she turned an opaque gaze toward us. "It's all rather strange, isn't it? Life goes on … until it doesn't. We had such a wonderfully easy life here. Now it seems like easy keeps getting harder every day."

Samantha leaned closer, reaching out to touch the woman's hand with shared commiseration, her own husband had been a victim of murder, and perhaps her brother-in-law as well.

"I had been staying at my sister's home," Mrs. Emsch told us. "Eddy insisted upon that. He was quite worried that something terrible might happen and wanted me away from here. It appears he was right. That evil woman in Hawaii killed him. I know that to be true like I know my own name. And it's my fault. I had contacted her and told her that any blackmail threats about exposing Eddy's fetishism or using that disgusting video were pointless. I told her that I knew all about it, so it was no longer a threat to him. Eddy was upset that I had spoken with her and worried that she might harm me after that. Next thing I knew, the police contacted me, and I rushed back here. I just honestly do not know what to do now."

"Did your husband ever say what might have happened to Gavin?" Samantha asked.

"Gavin?" Mrs. Emsch replied.

"Gavin was Cantu's husband. He's missing."

The widow then told us everything she knew that her husband had told her about Cantu soliciting Eddy to murder Gavin and how the police had been there asking questions about Gavin's disappearance. "But Eddy did not kill that man," she assured us. "He swore to me that he didn't."

It all made sense now, as much as any such set of such bizarre facts can. With Gavin dead Cantu would inherit, as his spouse, his sizeable fortune which, by the way, Gavin had inherited from his brother Griffin, when Griffin died – also murdered. Griffin's killer was currently serving time in prison, but it certainly seemed odd that Cantu was involved in both incidents. With a strong motive to have her husband killed, apparently Cantu then tried to blackmail Emsch into murdering Gavin by threatening to expose the humiliating video. Emsch declined. Perhaps Cantu, at that point, murdered Gavin herself or got someone else to do it. And then, since Emsch was going to testify against Cantu, she tried using the blackmail approach again, this time for his silence. Emsch and his wife called her bluff. The way I figured it, Cantu then murdered Emsch to silence him once and for all. How Cantu accomplished all that was up to law enforcement to determine, but all the main pieces of the puzzle finally fit together. Next stop was to share all this newly acquired information with the police.

CHAPTER THIRTY

The information eagerly given to the police by Ben Harding and Samantha Zimmer was not met with the importance they would have expected. An officer took their statements, a second officer asked them a few questions about how they ascertained their information, and they were sent on their way. This lukewarm reception infuriated Sammie, who continued to badger the police for further updates on a daily basis, and with all the determination of a bulldog, until she was told, in no uncertain terms, not to bother them again.

Ben suggested they contact Vincent Scatucci. "Vinnie's a former cop. Hell, not just a cop, he's a former FBI agent. Maybe he can get us an update somehow."

Only a few weeks later, Scatucci called Ben's cell phone.

"You have an update?" Ben asked anxiously.

"Oh, indeed I do," Scatucci answered. "I've got an update that you will not fucking believe."

Ben and Samantha arrived at Scatucci's office suite on Wilshire Boulevard in Beverly Hills. The elevator doors whispered open at level eleven, and they stepped through the aperture into the reception area. There was no one at the reception desk, but Ben knew his way around and led Sammie toward Vincent's office. Scatucci's door was open, and Ben could see his friend intently leafing through papers in a manilla file.

"Knock knock," Ben said announcing his arrival. "No receptionist, so we just let ourselves in."

"Oh good, you're here," Scatucci answered. "Come on in, *paesan*, have a seat. How ya doin' Samantha?"

"Yeah, I'm good," Sammie replied stroppily, finding herself sounding ungracious without fully meaning to. She harbored mixed feelings regarding Scatucci, finding his sexual innuendos and crude jokes repugnant, yet something about the man made him difficult not to like. And she certainly appreciated his counsel regarding her missing brother-in-law. Hoping to redeem herself with a kinder tone, she added, "Thank you so much for helping with this. I've been on pins and needles over this whole nasty thing. Anxious to hear what you've got for us."

They each took a seat in client chairs in front of the desk where Scatucci was seated.

"No Rivlen today either, huh?" Ben asked.

"Naw, the dude is on vacation for a few days," Scatucci answered. "Kinda quiet around here without him." Then the lawyer, former DEA agent, looked down at the file on his desk and began to narrate the gist of the information it contained. "It was in the early morning hours when Federal marshals boarded the yacht where Connie Cantu-Gambil lived and placed her under arrest for conspiracy to commit the murder of her husband. Bail was set at one million dollars. Since Cantu was denied access to her husband's bank accounts, she had no way to make bail."

Scatucci hesitated briefly, looking up over the file at the two seated before him. "But her incarceration would be brief."

"What the hell do you mean brief?" Samantha erupted with indignation. "She killed Gavin and that Emsch fellow. How could it be fucking brief?"

Scatucci continued. "The Monday after her arrest, less than a week behind bars, she was found dead in her cell."

Samantha let out an audible gasp, causing another momentary pause by Scatucci before going on.

"Autopsy results showed the cause of death to be asphyxiation. An object had been stuffed into her mouth and lodged in her throat, blocking her air intake. She suffocated and died." Again, Scatucci paused to let that information sink in. Then, "You should find this quite ironic. I know I did when I first read it earlier," he said. "The object, the official medical report states, was severed male genitals. A human penis and testicles."

"Jesus!" Ben exclaimed.

"Judging from the bruises on her arms and face, the medical examiner writes, the homicide was likely perpetrated by at least two killers. At least one person held her down and another stuffed the severed genitalia into her mouth, forced it down her throat, and held her mouth and nose shut, thereby cutting off her ability to take in air."

The three sat in silence for several moments, cogitating on the information they just learned. Samantha was the first to speak. "A perfectly fitting death for that cunt. Sorry for the language, but I couldn't have planned it better myself."

"Anyone want to wager what the DNA results will be as to where the genitalia came from?" Scatucci asked with a sarcastic tone.

"Oh, poor Mr. Emsch," Ben groaned.

"Poor Mrs. Emsch," Scatucci added. "I need to go out to Temecula and let her know what's in this report. It may be a while before she gets it through normal channels. It's the least I can do. That poor lady has gone through hell." What he could not divulge to his two friends seated in front of him, nor to Mrs. Emsch whenever he might visit her, was that he had recently acquired a new client whom he feared just may be at the heart of all of it.

## CHAPTER THIRTY-ONE

Randy Rivlen was exhausted. The eleven-hour flight from LAX to Charles de Gaulle Airport, made even longer when adding time elapsed for the plane to taxi between the gate and runway, plus Paris time being nine hours ahead of California, left him bleary-eyed and drained. A night in a comfortable Parisian hotel would be most welcome but was not on his itinerary. He had not yet reached his destination.

Walking thru customs, French officials stamped Rivlen's passport. He had a short downtime at de Gaulle, also known as Roissy Airport, before boarding a flight from Paris to Rome. He utilized the time between flights by using the rest room, sluicing his face with water in an effort to revive himself and rejoin the human race, grabbing some coffee, and gathering his luggage. Then he proceeded to the boarding area for his connecting flight.

The line to board the next plane was extremely long. After standing in line for what was beginning to seem like endless eternity, an airport employee pointed out that the line on the other side of the terminal was much shorter. Tired as he was, Rivlen was not all that keen to be lugging his bags across the terminal to the other line, so he said, "I just wanna stay in this line if you don't mind." But the employee *did* mind and was rather insistent, so Randy hauled his stuff over to the other line on the far side of the terminal. The line there, however, turned out to be even longer than the first line. Rivlen was instantly livid, cursing aloud about the sleezy French airport guy and how he must be purposely diverting American travelers to a longer line. Though Rivlen had never been to France before, he had heard tales of French rudeness toward Americans and was certain he had just experienced it first-hand.

It was a two-hour flight from Paris to Rome, then on to Naples. Many of the passengers boarding in Rome appeared to be business commuters just beginning their day and he was met with cheerful greetings by several. He just smiled in return, summoning whatever remaining energy he had. Rivlen had been traveling over sixteen straight hours and had little interest in the friendly chit-chat they tried to initiate. He was dog-tired.

The first thing Randy Rivlen noticed as he stepped off the plane in Naples was the stench. An odor that reminded him of dried urine assaulting his senses, and even though outdoors, it smelled like a filthy public restroom. The armpit of Italy someone on the plane had called Naples after Rivlen mentioned he was visiting for the first time. But another fellow passenger quickly came to the defense of Italy's third largest city. "To be the armpit of a place so beautiful as Italy is still a wondrous place to behold. I have been to Napoli many times. But I must tell you, be careful," the fellow warned, "a lot of crime. Mostly pickpockets. It happens just like that!" he said with authority, snapping his thumb and middle finger. "You reach for your wallet, and it is gone. But there are more dangerous people too. You must use caution walking the streets of Napoli. Especially if you are alone at night."

Rivlen gave a sleepy nod of appreciation for the warning.

"You will love Italy, I am sure," the passenger added, "but

why did you choose Napoli?"

Rivlen shrugged away an answer.

"Well, you should take the traghetti to Capri. Take in the splendor of *Grotta Azzurra*, the Blue Grotto. Or rent a vehicle and drive along the Amalfi Coast. There is so much to see, you will find the beauty of Italy at every turn."

Rivlen thanked him for the advice. So far, though, it was seeming as if the first man on the plane was right, it did seem like the armpit. Naples was dirty. Everywhere there were bins overflowing with trash and streets with rubbish piled up in the middle of the square. Walls covered with scrawled profanities, gardens full of weeds, historic-looking buildings seemingly falling apart.

Walking the street along the waterfront, seawalls and buildings were covered in graffiti. Statues standing outdoors in the open air that should be in museums, also defiled with graffiti. Works of art standing vigil over the piles of garbage that was littered everywhere. Rivlen had been to Tijuana, Mexico a couple times, another filthy city, but Naples, he decided, made Tijuana look like Beverly Hills by comparison.

Not just dirty but a seemingly hostile city as well. Everywhere he looked he saw people cursing and shaking fists at one another. He watched as a taxi driver drove dangerously close to several pedestrians, nearly running them down, then shook his fist at them, cursing in Italian as he sped away. Ironically, that same taxi was adorned with a crucifix and a large picture of Jesus; symbols of peace, love, and passivity.

But if hostility was pervasive in Napoli, coexisting right alongside of it was *amour*. Though, referring to the handy little English-to-Italian translation book he kept in his pocket, *amour*, he discovered, literally means a love affair that is kept secret. That would not be the correct term, because the *amour* he was witnessing was anything but secretive. Perhaps more appropriate would be the word passion. In the midst of the stench and graffiti there were lovers kissing, entwined in passionate embrace everywhere it seemed. At one corner bus stop Rivlen stood for several minutes watching a young couple in their twenties kissing goodbye. Kissing? Jesus, you could almost feel the high-octane lust-filled passion as you watched their tongues darting in and out of each other's mouths and their hands busily fondling each other. Whether hostile or passion, the *Neapolitans*, indeed, seemed to be a people of emotions.

And the traffic. Seeing how people drive here and how close pedestrians seem to come to death at each turn, Rivlen thought to himself, it makes sense that they would want to live in the moment.

Walking up a steep hill, he soon found himself in front of the address he had been given by his boss, Vincent Scatucci, and entered the apartment through a side door using the key given to him.

Closing the door and walking over to a window on the opposite wall, he looked out. There was a direct view of the harbor. A picturesque setting if it were not surrounded by filth and the ever-present graffiti. He could see a large boat with passengers boarding. Perhaps this was the traghetti ferry to Capri he had been told about.

To his left was a bar with bottles and glasses beckoning him. He poured himself a drink and reclined upon a comfortable-looking red sofa positioned in the middle of the room. Without even realizing it, a jet-lagged sleep enveloped him.

Several hours later he awoke, feeling like it was morning. He had no idea what time it was, but it was still dark outside. Looking out the window at the harbor, streetlights and ship lights glowed brightly, reflecting on the water.

His stomach growled. He felt hungry. The words of his in-flight friend that one should use caution walking the streets of Naples alone at night were outweighed by his need for food.

Strolling a few blocks along the street, he found a pizzeria and took a seat at an outdoor table. Placing an order with the waiter became a bit of a production because of the language barrier, but soon the mission was accomplished. *Napoletana*, the pizza of Naples, was smaller, flatter, and less perfectly round than American pizza, with a couple melted droppings of cheese, a dollop of red sauce, and a solitary basil leaf in the center as the only toppings. Not nearly as pretty as the pizza back home, he was thinking as he took a first bite. But it only took a single bite to discover it to be the absolute best pizza he had ever tasted. Quickly devouring the entire pie, he called the waiter over and ordered a second one. Two pizzas and several glasses of vino later, he was feeling pleasantly full.

With the contentment of a well-deserved slumber followed by *pizza e vino*, he began a walking exploration of the city. Wandering about the main streets of Napoli, he remained ever wary of the crime perpetrators he had been warned about but had, so far, not encountered. No overt acts of criminal intent, only clusters of rough-looking young Italians giving menacing looks to all who passed them by.

Pausing to stop at the entrance to a gothic-looking cathedral, he was struck by the sheer ornateness of the structure. Outside, sadly, its walls and doors were covered in graffiti. Not the hip street art that can give a neighborhood a contemporary atmosphere, this was the sort of in-your-face vandalism with sprayed names, pornographic depictions, and rude messages in both Italian and English. There was a young woman calmly standing just outside the church. "Ciao, sei americano?" she asked.

He understood just enough Italian to decipher what she had said. "Si," he responded. "Yes, I am American."

"My name is Patrizio," she said in suddenly perfect English. "Would you like to see inside?"

The classic set up, he thought. A lovely young girl enticing the unsuspecting American tourist to enter a place where he would surely be mugged – church or not. "No thank you," he answered. "Besides, I'm Jewish."

She gave an ominous laugh. "That's okay. You may still come inside and admire. You will find it the most grand church in all of Napoli. Grand yet elegant in its simplicity. Vast serenity with elegant stained-glass windows and an earthen-colored tiled floor. Very historical. Built in the 1300s but during World War II almost entirely destroyed by fire from an air raid. Rebuilt in the 1950s and returned to its former glory."

She sounded quite knowledgeable. Too much so. Like a tour guide with rehearsed speaking points. This had to be some sort of tempting trap. "No thanks. But thank you for the splendid information," he told her as he walked on.

Returning to the apartment, Rivlen set about the task he had been sent to do. Locating a short interior wall, exactly twenty feet to the left of the window overlooking the harbor, he gave a hard kick that cracked the plaster. A second kick opened a hole in the wall. More kicks expanded the hole. And then he saw it. A large black backpack that had been hidden inside the wall. He opened the pack. It overflowed with stacks of hundred-dollar bills, American money. This is what he had come for.

CHAPTER THIRTY-TWO

It was upon a white wooden Adirondack chair that Rose Emsch sat trancelike. In the distance, golden sun-bleached hillsides extending out beyond the verdure of nearly endless rows of thriving grapevines were being swallowed by late afternoon shadows, mottled patterns emerging, several slopes turning brown and sere, triggering a powerful sense of hiraeth in her very soul. The skeins of her thoughts were confusing, feeling trapped in a downward spiraling, diminishing, darkening place where the future didn't exist, and the present made no sense. Her husband was dead, yet that seemed impossible for her to grasp. More impossible still, the *way* he died. Brutally murdered, mutilated, dismembered. She shivered, trying to purge the imagery.

How could a life together that felt so perfect come to such a tragic end? People say there is no such thing as a perfect marriage, but theirs was. They had a perfect marriage. As a young woman, she had dated and waited for the exact right man to arrive in her life. And, when he did, she was ready. It was love at first sight, well nearly. By their third date she knew he was the one. He may not have been the most handsome man but there was a rugged, yet tender, self-confidence that was alluring. What he may have lacked in masculine pulchritude – an ugly word that means beauty – he was most definitely a man's man. An alpha male. At least that is what she always thought for the more than dozen years they had been together.

Ruing her discovery of the strange perversions he harbored for so long without her ever being aware, urges that drove him to employ the services of a distant facilitator that ultimately led to his demise. Why had he not trusted in her enough to confide such fetishes? Would she have been accepting had he done so? Would she have engaged in his strange desires, thereby removing the necessity of finding someone else to fulfill his needs? If he had, and if she did, she might not be sitting out here alone banging her head against the sky. The perfect life they shared would not have crashed and burned the way it did. The most bitter regret of all, however, was in searching out that horrible woman in Hawaii, calling her on the phone, threatening her. That had proven to be a most egregious error. So, in the final analysis, was it really Rose's own fault? Was *she* ultimately to blame for the horrendous turn of events?

Suddenly realizing she was verbalizing her thoughts, hearing them aloud, not just in her head, she scrambled for a way to stop speaking before starting to perseverate like some crazy woman in a psychiatric ward. "Why!" her final agonized *cri de coeur* screamed into the open fields populated only by rows of grapevines. Then a morose mewl as she began to sob uncontrollably, "Why, why, why?"

# CHAPTER THIRTY-THREE

It was daylight now. Randy Rivlen sat in the Napoli apartment on a large red sofa in the center of the room, counting stacks of paper money while consuming the contents of a bottle of *Nonino grappa* appropriated from the bar. Occasional glances through the window at the glistening sunlight on the sea got him to thinking. Daydreaming. Just a relatively short distance across that body of water is Monaco, the gambling Mecca of this part of the world. Fuck Capri and its lagoons, Monaco was a place he had always wanted to go. A bucket list item.

Opening a second bottle of grappa, the alcoholic buzz settling over him, and feeling the lure of all that money now in his possession, he began imagining what it would be like to lay down a few bets at Monte Carlo. What a dream experience that would be. The gravitational pull of such a place was overpowering.

Rivlen, an admitted gambling addict, knew he should be careful with such thoughts. But wasn't he entitled to realize such a dream? He had been Scatucci's beast of burden for too many years. Doing the boring, down-and-dirty work, nose pressed to a computer screen or in law books researching case law, writing legal briefs, while Scatucci got all the glory. Scatucci putting on his thespian lawyer show for judges and juries in courtrooms, getting interviewed on TV, getting laid by gorgeous women who thought he was so smart and cool. Scatucci always the star entertainer while his law clerk played the behind-the-scenes straight man. Well, maybe now it was Rivlen's turn. A few well-placed bets, a bit of luck, and he might even double the money in the backpack. Return the original amount to his boss and keep the rest for himself. Begin a brand-new life. Then he could tell Scatucci to go fuck himself.

## CHAPTER THIRTY-FOUR

# BEN HARDING

As I entered the beach house Sammie was nowhere to be seen. She had her own key now and we had arranged to meet for dinner. I'd been delayed and, anticipating she would have arrived before me, expected to see her. Perhaps she was on the front deck enjoying the view. But no, she wasn't there. I remained a few moments embracing the last lingering rays of sun as it was being devoured by the encroaching fog, followed by gathering chill.

Returning indoors, I called out and searched all the rooms of the house, but she was nowhere to be found. Figuring I must have somehow arrived before her, I poured myself a glass of cabernet and started heading back outside toward the deck … when I sensed movement a few feet away inside the living room, near the large old fireplace, causing me to momentarily freeze. Suddenly, I realized the huge soft down comforter on the overstuffed couch was moving. I walked in that direction. It was Samantha, turning in her sleep. I had completely missed her enveloped in the bulky blanket. I stood looking down at her asleep. It struck me as nice, somehow, that she felt so comfortable in my home as to let herself in and take a nap. She looked so peaceful I was hesitant to disturb her. Then her eyes fluttered. She saw me standing over her and smiled up at me.

"Hi you," I quietly greeted.

"Oh, hey. Hi," her voice groggy, raspy. "You're here. How long was I asleep?"

"Don't know," I told her. "I just got home. But I might have let you go on sleeping through dinner. You probably could use the rest with all that's been going on."

"It was nice. The sound of the ocean waves so relaxing, caused me to doze off. I wasn't really all that tired, just needed a break from my own thoughts, I guess."

"Well, we don't need to go out. We can have a relaxing dinner right here," I said, putting on some music. Classical piano, the andante movement of the piece I knew to be one of her favorites fit with the mood. "I'll light a fire and we can eat right here in front of the fireplace. Good?"

"In the words of the legendary Greek philosopher Mediocrates, *Ehh, good enough*," she joked.

"Gee, here I am trying to set up a nice romantic atmosphere and all I get are wisecracks?"

"I'm sorry. It's a coverup. Truth is, I feel more like crying right now than laughter. I am so bloody angry at that Hawaiian woman and what I fear has happened to poor Gavin."

"I know," I said in my most empathetic voice.

"All I can think about is extracting vengeance on that terrible woman."

I smiled, shaking my head.

"Wait, why are you giving me that look?" she asked with modulated intonation.

"Because you mean *exact*, not *extract*. When you extract

something, you remove it. Exact, when used as a verb, means to require or demand."

She moved to a sitting up position on the couch, staring at me blankly in feigned astonishment. "So instead of consoling me, you give me a fucking language lesson? Okay, yes! Exact is *exactly* what I meant." Lucky for me she was now smiling, and I was glad my segue had caused it. "Now make a fire, pour me some wine, sit here next to me and let's see what else I might learn from you tonight."

CHAPTER THIRTY-FIVE

Randy Rivlen's imagined new life was over. His old life was over too. There was no way to repair the damage done, and he had only himself to blame. He'd always had a gambling addiction and should have known better. In the past he had lost money doing sports betting. And in Las Vegas he had been a regular. But this was the big time: Monaco. Like going from smoking marijuana to injecting heroin. The highest of highs. The high that not only comes from the thrill of betting, but the intoxicating atmosphere of the entire gambling scene. Indulging always took him to a whole other level of consciousness, one where he lost all connection to anything outside of placing bets, becoming completely absorbed in the gambling activities and pursuing them in an uncontrollable compulsive manner, despite any potential negative repercussion.

He had tried his best to stop. It was only after his conviction for embezzlement, a crime he committed to finance his gambling addiction, that he was finally able to rein it in. Before that, win or lose, he had enjoyed every minute of his addiction. But becoming a convicted felon, that was rock bottom.

Prison afforded the opportunity to study law, something at which he became somewhat proficient, but his felony conviction would forever prevent him from becoming a real lawyer. Vinnie Scatucci became his savior, giving him a chance to use those legal skills at a time when no one else would, helping him hone those skills to a higher level of competency. And now, just like a modern-day Judas Iscariot, he had betrayed his savior.

But Vinnie was even more than that. Vinnie had become a close friend. Perhaps the closest friend Randy ever had. Both of them sports nuts, they often hung out together after work at a local sports bar, tipping back beers and watching ball games on the TV above the bar. He loved Vincent Scatucci like a brother. But having all that cash in his possession and finding himself a stone throw from the most famous gambling arena in the world had proven too much to resist. Like putting a drug addict in a room filled with drugs. To say gambling is as addictive as drugs would be an understatement. In fact, gambling addiction, Randy knew, was the most common impulse control disorder worldwide. Now he had succumbed, fallen off the wagon, and his life was over.

The evening was pleasantly cool in contrast to the heat of the day when he arrived in Monaco. The outline of Monte Carlo was silhouetted against the evening sky, the shore lights reflecting on the smooth surface of the sea, mingling with the mirrored beams from boats moving silently back and forth across the bay. Monaco, a dramatically minuscule nation tacked onto the bottom of France along the picturesque French Riviera, is the world's second smallest country – the only country smaller is the Vatican – with some of the most idyllic beach settings to be found anywhere and a legendary harbor serving hundreds of mega-yachts floating in the water. But he had not come for the beaches. It was the high-end casinos and stifling amount of money on display that drew him in.

Bizarrely, someone informed him upon arrival, if you are a resident of Monaco, you are not allowed to gamble in the nation's luxurious casinos. Allegedly, the government wants its residents to *not* squander their wealth in a casino, but tourists are more than welcome to gamble. Living here and not being allowed to gamble, he surmised, would be like a Catholic priest sworn to celibacy living in the Playboy Mansion filled with beautiful starlets.

The Monte Carlo Casino, officially named Casino de Monte-Carlo, was an amazing gambling complex. Complete with all attendant opulence, Monaco's most exclusive gambling venue. This is truly what heaven must look like, he thought when first setting eyes on the magnificent Taj Mahal-like structure. Inside, the casino patrons were all dressed to the nines, looking every bit the wealthy jet-set. But to his surprised delight, he found the minimum bets at Casino de Monte-Carlo to be quite affordable, with most games starting at just five euros. The highest end of the spectrum was blackjack, requiring a minimum bet of twenty-five euros, followed closely by Punto-Banco, with a minimum bet of twenty euros. Not only did this place *look* like heaven, it was, indeed, heaven.

He wasted no time making the rounds, betting larger and larger sums of money on blackjack, craps, poker, as well as roulette and even slot machines. Dopamine being released from the reward center of his brain like a rushing river of intoxication. With alarming speed, he blew through most of the retainer money he had been instructed to deliver to Scatucci.

Finally coming down from his gambling high and realizing the magnitude of what he had done, he became immersed in depression. In the absence of any viable alternative, he drafted a short letter on hotel stationery confessing what he had done and folded it into a corresponding envelope. Addressing the envelope to Scatucci's office and placing it in the mail, he contemplated suicide as his only option. There was no way he could ever return to the States, to California. Unless ….

## CHAPTER THIRTY-SIX

Scatucci had an uneasy feeling about representing Rojas Raton. Though Vinnie was well-known for defending people arrested on drug charges, Raton possibly – probably – having something to do with Emsch's death was something Vinnie found troubling and could not seem to shake. Could the quarter million retainer fee curb those dubious misgivings?

He tried to rationalize that Raton was not charged with any homicide and there was no proof that he had murdered anyone. He was only being held on drug related charges. To that end, Raton was entitled to the best defense available under the laws of the great state of California. And Vinnie was the man for that job. He was, after all, in the business of providing legal defense for those finding themselves in such situations. It was his *duty* to provide the best defense possible.

All this was going through his mind as he sat in a dentist's chair, the hygienist probing around inside his mouth with her tools. "Too much plaque," he heard her say, interrupting his ruminations. "I don't think you've been flossing enough. How often do you floss?" Her question perturbed him. How could she expect a patient to answer when her fingers, some cotton, and a metal instrument were in his mouth? He tried to mumble some sort of acknowledgement but, before he could, she added, "You may want to consider buying a Waterpik too."

Leaving the dentist's office, driving his Ferrari along Beverley Boulevard, turning onto North Canon Drive, then pulling into a public parking structure, he was running a few minutes late for his haircut appointment. Gornik & Drucker was more than just a place for getting your hair coifed. It was a true California experience, a long-time fixture in the Golden Triangle and part of Beverly Hills culture. Vinnie enjoyed the sophisticated ambience of the place with its wood-paneled interior while getting a traditional hot towel shave and a trim. One of the many little indulgences he could afford as a lawyer, and far preferable to the Super Cuts days when he was a cop.

An hour later, with clean teeth, a close shave, and fresh haircut, he was back in the whining red Italian sport car, feeling like a freshly minted million dollars. Turning off Wilshire Boulevard, up a ramp leading to the outdoor third floor of a mirrored office complex and pulling into a parking spot with his name painted on it, he shut down the car. The whining of the engine stopped.

Vincent Scatucci had a spring in his step as he got off the elevator on the eleventh floor and headed for his office. Evelyn, his current receptionist/secretary in a long line of prior receptionist/secretaries, brought in a stack of mail and placed it on his desk. "My, you look especially dapper today," she commented. "You smell very nice, too."

Evelyn had been with Scatucci a little over a year. In her mid-twenties, this was her first employment as a legal secretary. Vinnie found her a little ditzy but efficient enough. Mostly, she had a great telephone voice and when clients came into the office, who often were nervous and on edge from being charged with a crime and meeting with a lawyer, she had a way of making them feel relaxed and comfortable. She could be flirty at times, including with her boss, and while Vinnie had wondered more than a few times what it might be like to have sex with her, he made it a rule never to frolic with office staff. Paralegal Rivlen, however, openly lusted for Evelyn, practically drowning in his own drool every time she came near him. It got to the point where Vinnie had to lay down the law. "There are plenty of other women out there in the world, Randy. Literally thousands right here in Beverly Hills. And I'm not using literally figuratively, I'm using literally *literally*. Thousands! No need to hit on this one just because you can. No need to create sexual tension here in the workplace."

Rivlen gave him a helpless look. Easy for Scatucci to mandate such dictum. He was out and about in the limelight every day, hobnobbing with beautiful ladies all over L.A. while Randy was stuck inside the office working with his nose in a law book.

"Got it?" Vincent warned.

"Got it, boss," Randy had answered begrudgingly. "Don't shit where you eat. Yep, got it."

"Thank you, Evelyn," the lawyer said, picking up a white letter sized envelope from atop the stack. The envelope had an ornate hotel logo and foreign postmark. Using a Mont Blanc letter opener to slice it open, and removing the single page from within, it was a brief handwritten note.

"Let me know if you need anything else," Evelyn replied seeing him reading the letter as she made her exit.

"Wait," Scatucci called to her before she had cleared the door.

Reentering. "Yes sir?" She noticed a pained look on her boss' face.

"Oh ... um ... never mind. Shut my door will you please,

Evelyn?"

"Of course," she complied with a smile.

He crumpled the handwritten single page letter and held it in his fist. The million-dollar mood he enjoyed just minutes ago evaporated. A vein at his right temple began throbbing and suddenly his whole head felt as if it might explode. He never should have sent Rivlen to retrieve the filthy lucre in Italy. What an amazingly stupid thing to do. Spinning his chair around to stare out the window behind his desk, he could see the traffic below along the Wilshire corridor. Merely a few sparse words scrawled on a piece of hotel stationery, the message would create a life altering event.

CHAPTER THIRTY-SEVEN

Five-thirty on a carefree California Sunday. Early morning. Rubbing sleep from his eyes, Ben Harding sipped coffee from a mug adorned with yacht club burgees and looked out at the dawning new day. The ocean was like glass: smooth, barely a ripple. The sun was just rising above the nearby inland cliffs, mists of lingering fog clinging stubbornly to the land, the air remaining chilled. This was, perhaps, Ben's favorite time of day. The world was not yet out and about. He only shared the beach with lolling sea lions floating carelessly in the water or relaxing upon the sand; pelicans gracefully gliding in formation mere inches above the ocean's watery surface in search of prey; along with sea gulls, their voices sounding like laughter, giddy at the prospect of an early morning fish-fest breakfast.

Ben was pulling on his running shoes and heading out, creating the first footprints in the pristine sand. He loved his morning jogs along the beach where the ocean water greets the shore, though running on the soft dry sand offered a much more difficult workout than running on the damp compacted sand. If he was being completely honest with himself, and just now he *was* being completely honest with himself – after all it was Sunday – he had to admit he had become somewhat of an exercise addict. Morning jogs were often followed by a swim, surfing, or perhaps a couple hours of kayaking. He'd never been to a gym in his life, but these daily activities had given him an envious physique: lean and muscular.

Finishing a two-mile run, then dragging his kayak down the sandy beach to the water's edge, jumping onto the orange fiberglass sit-atop boat, he launched it into the ocean. Dolphins began leaping with early morning vigor nearby. The world, this world, his world, was a beautiful place. Heading the mile or so toward the breakwater and jetty just outside the marina, some fishing boats were venturing out to sea. He paddled past the breakwater, rounding the rocky barriers like a gymkhana barrel racer, then paddled hard against the outgoing tide toward the marina.

Ben loved paddling in and out of the dock fingers inside the marina, looking at myriad boats resting peacefully in their slips. Especially the sailboats, with their low sleek lines and tall masts reaching toward the sky, enticing sailors with dreams of tradewinds taking them to faraway places. But all boats were not created equal. Just like people, some were too wide, some too top-heavy, some blemished and poorly maintained, and a few just plain ugly. But, he decided, most were beautiful, and a precious few downright breathtaking.

There was one such vessel that Ben spotted. Slowing his paddling in order to linger, examining and appreciating the slender lines of the double-ender hull. Probably not the most impressive boat in the marina by yachtie standards, but something about this sailboat just appealed to Ben's nautical taste buds. Again, just like with people, there was a certain chemistry that connected man with boat, sometimes for no apparent reason. This one perhaps thirty-six feet in length, solid looking, rigged for blue water cruising. The name painted on both sides near the stern read *BODACIOUS* and listed her home port as Marina del Rey.

Eight o'clock now and the morning was warming up, so he removed his rash-guard shirt as he squeezed part-way into the slip, maneuvering the slender kayak alongside *Bodacious*. He was looking upward, inspecting the tall mast and rigging when a female voice startled him.

"Hello?" the voice asked, sounding accusatory.

Squinting into the sun, holding a hand above his eyes as a visor, Ben could barely make out a woman's face shrouded in sunlight, looking down at him from the foredeck. He shouldn't have squeezed so close, surely an invasion of privacy. "Sorry," he replied. "Just admiring your boat. Didn't mean to intrude. Didn't see you up there."

"You like what you see?" the voice responded, now with a tinge of playfulness.

"The more I look, the more I like," Ben told the face whose features were just coming into focus in the glaring sunlight, hoping the double entendre wasn't pushing it. As his eyes adjusted he could see she was young and pretty, lying tummy down, sunbathing, bikini top unfastened to avoid tan lines. And she was smiling, so apparently he'd not exceeded any bounds.

"Oh, I know what that's like," she said, even more playful now. "I've been lying here watching you paddle up the channel."

Several minutes of banter turned to chat. An easy conversant that added to her overall attractiveness. She was now sitting upright, bikini top re-fastened, barely covering milky white breasts that contrasted sharply against the rest of her bronzed self and threatening to pop out of confinement. The name of the boat, coupled with the view Ben was enjoying, reminded him of a line from a movie, *a pair of Bodacious ta-tas*, causing him to chuckle.

"What's so amusing?" the girl onboard demanded with mock severity.

Ben continued sitting idly atop the kayak, paddle draped across his legs, not sure how to respond. "Oh, nothing really," he said, shaking his head. Searching for something to keep the conversation going, he added, "Says Marina del Rey on your stern."

"I knew you were checking out my stern!" She said laughing.

Stammering a bit, while laughing at the same time, "No, I mean … well, I live in Del Rey, too. Venice Beach, actually." A momentary lull in the chat, then Ben added, "So, you live aboard?"

"Oh gosh, no. It's my dad's boat. He's the sailor. I just hang here on weekends sometimes."

Her dad's boat. Another young one. To Ben, another reminder of his advanced age. Time to move along. "Well, have a nice rest of your day, and don't forget to tan both sides evenly."

Paddling his kayak past one of the waterfront eateries, he watched people enjoying Sunday brunch on an outdoor patio. Two attractive mid-forties ladies, spotting the tanned, shirtless kayaker, raised their mimosas in his direction and waved. A bit more age-appropriate Ben thought to himself as he sheepishly waved back, missing a stroke of paddling in the process. He knew his sun-browned body and the way the paddling motion naturally flexed his muscles was something women appreciated, much as a long-legged female in a short skirt is fully aware of the admiring glances she gets from men as she passes. Ben could not deny that he enjoyed the attention, but always seemed to be taken by surprise each time it occurred. Perhaps due to the twenty years he spent as a bloated, out-of-shape, desk-bound lawyer who never got such attention – before quitting the mega-firm where he'd slaved his way up to low-level partner and became reborn as an actual human being.

The day warmed on, ten o'clock and seventy-three degrees now. Returning home to a breakfast of eggs and juice out on his beachfront deck, he sat and people watched. Active people. Happy people. Young and old. Walking, jogging, pushing baby strollers, trotting behind leash-tugging canines, bicycle riders, skateboarders, roller-bladers. Even the old and infirm, ambling along with assistance from ski pole-like sticks for guidance, sometimes on the arm of a caretaker. Almost all with smiling faces and pleasant greetings as they pass one another, "Lovely day." The sort of day that, in Ben's estimation, made life truly worth living. Absolutely no way Benjamin Harding could have guessed the peace and tranquility of his world would soon be shattered.

# CHAPTER THIRTY-EIGHT

Vincent Scatucci sat upright in bed after a fitful, sleepless night. Was it only ten days ago that he felt on top of his game, walking on air, able to sleep soundly through the night? Now his life had been turned upside down. Each day more stress-filled. Outside his bedroom window the new-day sun glistened on the ocean water. The sun always seemed to shine in Southern California, even at the most inopportune times. It was truly a wonderous place to live. He'd been happy here the past fifteen years since leaving the Midwest … and since his divorce. He'd watched his daughter grow up here, more or less, one weekend a month and three weeks every summer. Gina had matured into a fine young woman, notwithstanding growing up in a divided family. God, he loved his daughter so. For twenty-one years Gina had remained the finest thing in his life. He would do absolutely anything to protect her from harm.

Did he have any regrets? Certainly. He regretted making mistakes. But he was a man who usually appreciated his regrets, learned from them. But the mistake that was now occupying his mind was in a league all its own, and his regret on a whole new level.

Pushing himself from bed and walking purposefully down

the stairway that emptied into his kitchen, Scatucci poured himself some coffee. Lifting the mug to his lips and blowing across the rim, he took a seat at the breakfast bar, dumping two bales of shredded wheat into a bowl, dousing it with milk. A couple bites and he decided to finish breakfast outside on the patio.

This was a perfect perch from which to observe beach life, a microcosm of real life. Joggers plodded along the sand. The same familiar faces he saw most mornings. They waved as they passed, Vinnie returning their salutation without really paying attention. He breathed deep the damp viscous ocean air, momentarily holding it in his lungs before expelling it with an audible sigh. Some people were playing a morning game of volleyball a bit farther out on the beach. He stayed on the patio watching their game for a long while. That's what life really is, a fast moving game, he determined. A game nobody really wins because in the end we all die. Since there is no way of winning, the best one can hope for is to simply enjoy playing the game while it lasts.

Perhaps, though, life's game is actually more like a chess match. Less physically strenuous, more serious, requiring greater strategy. One must be thinking clearly before executing each move lest it beget serious setback. A single imprudent move and the king goes down: match over. Doesn't matter who was ahead prior. At that point the board is cleared, with both king and pawn returning to the same box.

A woman walking her dog extends a good morning greeting as she passes. He answers with only a nod. Is it a good morning? Maybe ... but the rest of the day, mighty doubtful. Her dog is tethered to her by a long retractable leash. The dog looks old. A liver and white Springer Spaniel with matted fur, gray around its muzzle, and a crusty goop formed at its eyes. Long floppy ears swaying to its slow elderly cadence, the dog suddenly strikes an odd stance, its stubby docked tail erect. Defecating. The woman, dutifully pulling a bag from her pocket, bends over to pick up the poop. He wonders, is she always so conscientious or did she pick it up only because he was watching?

His coffee cup empty and the uneaten cereal in the bowl now mushy, he sauntered back inside to the kitchen, placing the bowl in the sink and pouring a second cup of joe. A clock in the shape of a coffee pot with the words Tempus Fugit emblazoned on it hangs on the wall above the pantry. He glances up, eight o'clock. Time enough to finish his second cup and further deliberate toward a conclusion on how he will execute the rest of his day.

He has a very important meeting to attend in just a few hours. One might even call it a *life-altering* meeting. The subject of which had been stressfully occupying his thoughts to near exclusivity for the last many days, taking him from agitation, to anger, to rage. Also, fear. But this morning there was equilibrium. A different trajectory, a sense of aplomb, accepting what he knew must be done.

Strolling back to the bedroom, coffee mug in hand, and opening the clothes closet, he stood looking absently at the array of business suits hanging there in neat arrangement. Gray suit? No, probably should go darker, he decided. The right tie adding a splash of color. Dozens of neckties were suspended from a circular turnstile. He gave the tie-wheel a spin, like a contestant on Wheel of Fortune, and plucked one off the ring. Holding the silky garment in his hands, he smiled. It was a Nicole Miller. A brightly colored novelty-type tie with a lawyer theme that Gina had given him for his birthday several years ago, displaying the scales of justice, law books, and the words Criminal Law. His smile evolved to a grin. "Perfect."

The meeting was in nearby Century City at a lawyer's office. Scatucci was personally unfamiliar with this lawyer, other than he had a reputation as a good negotiator and was supposedly good at dispute resolution. Paralegal and former law clerk Randy Rivlen had arranged the meeting with this lawyer because Rivlen *needed* an expert at dispute resolution. To say Rivlen and Scatucci had a dispute in need of resolution would be a gross understatement. Rivlen had misappropriated a quarter million dollars of client funds, informing his boss of it in a mere single-page letter, apologizing for his *transgression*. The letter Scatucci had read days earlier at his office, written on stationery emblazoned with a fancy logo from a luxury hotel in Monaco. It made Scatucci furious. Then he was contacted by this damn lawyer who claimed Rivlen had hired him to help work things out and save their relationship. Scatucci knew this meeting with a lawyer was not going to save anyone.

He returned to the kitchen, setting the coffee mug down on a counter, then rummaging around in a drawer next to where he was seated for something to write with, put pen to paper and drafted a letter of his own. A letter he hoped would be discovered by the intended recipient. A letter of explanation. A letter of goodbye. Then he showered and dressed, completed a few quick errands, a stop at the bank to add something to his safe deposit box, and proceeded to the dreaded meeting with Rivlen and his solicitor.

Arriving at the Century Plaza Twin Towers, their gleaming aluminum skinned triangular shapes standing as the tallest landmark for miles, he parked the black BMW in what a sign proclaimed as the world's largest underground parking garage, offering over 5,000 spots.

Wearing his best dark blue suit, Nicole Miller lawyer tie, and carrying a fat briefcase, Vincent Scatucci walked into the lawyer's office on the seventh floor of the forty-four storied Century City structure. Standing near the receptionist's desk, he waited patiently as she disappeared through a door, promising to "be right back." A tune from the office Muzak system wafted almost imperceptibly through the airwaves, Phil Collins' haunting voice: *I can feel it coming in the air tonight – Oh Lord.* Vincent sighed heavily. Oh Lord indeed, he thought morbidly to himself, I most surely *can* feel it coming in the air.

The receptionist quickly returned and led him into one of the interior offices. Vincent took a seat not too near his unscrupulous former law clerk and across the desk from the attorney. Sunlight streamed in through an impressive floor to ceiling window overlooking the city. The bright sun was inappropriate, Vincent decided. Gray and gloomy would be more fitting for this day.

Alone in the room with these two, suddenly Vincent's heart was racing, sweat dripped from his forehead, the pits of his suit jacket becoming visibly damp. The lawyer, seated at his desk, was rifling through some documents that had apparently been prepared in advance of this meeting. Finally, the lawyer looked up, all smiles and entreaty, his squinty eyes crinkling at the corners, and made an initial attempt at small talk, apparently trying to set the mood toward a more amiable encounter, or at least a reduction of hostility. Randy Rivlen writhed in his seat with obvious discomfort. His visage screaming guilt and remorse. He offered an affected smile toward Scatucci that went unreciprocated.

And then the anticipated negotiations began. Though hardly a negotiation since Scatucci merely sat listening quietly as Rivlen's lawyer spoke. With carefully curated finesse he laid out a plan and presented it to Scatucci. The crux of it being that, as recompense, Rivlen would repay the stolen money – a quarter million dollars – with modicum interest, over the course of several years.

Rivlen looked directly at Scatucci with pleading watery eyes.

"I am so sorry, Vinnie. I don't know what came over me. You know I have a gambling addiction. I just cannot help myself. I did not mean for this to happen. Please believe me. You have no idea how much this has been tearing me up inside. So much so that suicide was high on my list of how to deal with all this. But I decided I owe you more than to merely take the coward's way out. So, I'm here today falling on my sword. After all you have done for me, the least I can do is be man enough to face you. Thank you for coming today and meeting with us. I know you will never be able to trust me again, but I promise to pay it all back. I swear."

"Yeah? Pay it back? How's that gonna work? You're a fucking loser. An ex con. How is it that you're gonna repay me?" The bitter derision in Scatucci's voice caused Rivlen to look away, hanging his head.

The lawyer then spoke again. "I have agreed to hire Mr. Rivlen as head law clerk here at my firm. He has agreed for seventy-five percent of his wages to be paid directly to you, Mr. Scatucci, until the debt is paid in full."

Scatucci sat staring straight ahead, nonresponsive, acknowledging neither of the other two men in the room.

"Additionally, he has agreed to place his residence up for sale with one hundred percent of the proceeds of the sale to be paid directly to you. It's a modest home, and heavily mortgaged, but with the way the market is right now, and with so much of his wages going to you, I think you can expect to be paid within three years."

Scatucci continued his stare into some middle distance of space. "Three years," he repeated, his voice a soft whisper.

"Do you think this may be workable, Mr. Scatucci?" the lawyer asked. "Quite frankly, this sounds like a fair deal to me," he added. "Unless you may have some alternative ideas for repayment."

Turning his head slowly, Scatucci looked from the lawyer to Rivlen and back again to the lawyer. Locking eyes with him but saying nothing.

"This is a reasonable and fair offer," the lawyer reiterated. "But if there is some counteroffer you would like to make, this is the time to do it."

Vincent Scatucci was looking past the lawyer, through him, to the enormous window directly behind, appreciating the blue sky just beyond as if it were something he might never see again.

"Reasonable? Fair?" Scatucci at last spoke, his voice hoarse but fractious. Picking up his briefcase and balancing it on his lap, "Here's what I think is fair. Let me show you my counteroffer." Reaching his hand deep into the briefcase, fidgeting for the .38 caliber handgun he'd brought to the meeting, the glint of a gun barrel caught his errant former law clerk's eye. It was the last thing Randy Rivlen would ever see. There was a loud, percussive pop. A bullet smashed into Rivlen's skull, toppling him over in his chair, splattering blood and parts of his brain onto the lawyer's expensive Persian rug covering the office floor.

The lawyer shrieked, "What the …!"

Scatucci turned a glassy-eyed stare toward the cowering lawyer. Instantly fearing for his own life, the lawyer ducked under the desk. Scatucci looked away, back toward his former law clerk lying dead on the floor, knowing what he had to do next. He had grappled with this consequence long before even arriving at the lawyer's office. Only one choice. He must pay for what he just did, and as a former cop, former DEA agent, and well-known lawyer, prison was not an option. He took a deep breath, put the gun to his own temple, and pulled the trigger.

## CHAPTER THIRTY-NINE

# BEN HARDING

It was a Wednesday morning that I will not soon forget. A typically bright, beautiful California beach day. Eighty-two degrees with sunlight sparkling like diamonds off the Pacific as I cruised my way along Pacific Coast Highway with the top down on the Porsche. My cell phone rang, the roaring sound of the wind as I drove made it difficult to hear the caller. In fact, I don't even remember now who it was that called but, whoever it was, that's where I first heard the devastating news.

At first, I thought it was a joke. A really bad joke. Too impossible to believe. I pulled into the lot at Norm's Coffee Shop, popped some quarters into the slot of a newspaper vending machine and pulled out the paper. The strange and tragic event involving my friend was front page news. The headline read like a pulp murder mystery:

# DEAD KILLER IDENTIFIED AS BEVERLY HILLS ATTORNEY

In an apparent murder/suicide, the lawyer who shot and killed a business associate and then killed himself has been identified as Vincent G. Scatucci, a Los Angeles criminal defense attorney and former federal drug agent who was well known in the legal community and to the general public for high-profile criminal cases, most recently in the news for his recent representation of celebrity madam Bambini Bella.

Attorney Scatucci was attending a settlement conference at another attorney's office in Century City when negotiations turned ugly. Police said Scatucci, 52, of Marina del Rey shot and killed Randy Rivlen, 54, a paralegal, after they argued over a business matter in the Century City law office. According to a police description, Scatucci pulled a handgun from his briefcase, pointed it at Rivlen, his own law clerk, shot and killed him. Scatucci then put the gun to his own head and pulled the trigger, ending his life.

Former clients and colleagues of Scatucci said they were at a loss to explain his behavior. A colleague who prefers to remain anonymous described Scatucci as a "Wonderful guy. Warm-hearted and gregarious. The kind of guy everybody liked. Funny and witty but with a total take-no-prisoners courtroom style. Highly skilled at impeaching prosecution witnesses. On cross examination he was a total shark."

In Scatucci's Beverly Hills' office, still brimming with piles of legal documents stacked several feet high on the floor, office assistant Evelyn Nelson, 24, called the situation simply unbelievable. "Vinnie was a really good boss," she is quoted as saying. "This was my very first job working in a law office and he taught me a lot. I will really miss him. And Randy too. He was also very nice."

My knees went weak, I sat down abruptly onto the concrete curb, the newspaper falling to the ground. The news story defied everything I ever thought I knew about my friend Vinnie Scatucci. The guy I knew had never been prone to violence, never. In fact, he left law enforcement to escape the violence he encountered in that job. He was a guy who genuinely seemed to love his life, certainly not at all self-destructive. That Vinnie could suddenly kill both himself and Randy Rivlen was completely unimaginable.

So unimaginable, in fact, that the next day I drove into the city for a chat with the investigating police detective assigned to Scatucci's case.

"Investigation is still ongoing, so I cannot really comment much, but I gotta tell ya, for all intents and purposes, this case is basically closed," the detective told me. "This was a murder/suicide with an eyewitness to the entire thing. A witness who just happens to be the other lawyer who was in the room at the time of the shooting."

"I checked Scatucci's day planner," I argued with the cop. "He had his teeth cleaned just days before. Who the hell gets their teeth cleaned and then decides to kill themselves?"

The cop sat at his desk absently chewing on a number 2 pencil. Whether what I was saying penetrated his consciousness I could not really determine.

"A very expensive shave and haircut from some fancy men-only salon, too. What? He just wanted to look and feel his best before blowing his face off?"

"What can I tell you?" the detective replied, removing the pencil from his teeth but barely looking up. "Like I said, this case is still under investigation, but all things considered it seems pretty cut and dried." As I turned to leave, I swear I heard the cop mumble, "One less turncoat cop criminal defense lawyer ain't exactly a tragedy."

Outraged, I drove by the lawyer/witness' office in Century City. He did not seem at all pleased to see me. Perhaps he was just tired of talking about what must have been a truly horrific ordeal for him, or maybe it was something more. The way I was given the bum-rush out of his office caused me to wonder if he had something to hide. I was suddenly suspicious of everyone and everything.

Days later, Scatucci's funeral service – if one might call it such, because it more closely resembled a fun social gathering, more celebratory than somber – was held outdoors, high on a hotel rooftop in Marina del Rey, offering views below of yachts snug in their expensive slips and the endless blue Pacific in the distance. Come to pay their respects was a group of roughly fifty-plus mourners all wearing the clothes of professionals, seated at round tables with white tablecloths, consuming quantities of alcoholic beverages and catered hotel food.

Just like me, no one could come to grips with the violent manner in which Scatucci's life ended. "It just doesn't make sense," one fellow-mourner told me. "Vinnie and Randy were more than just coworkers. They were friends, for Christ's sake. They went to baseball games together. They hung out together after work. For this to happen is way beyond bizarre. It's the most far-fetched thing I ever would have imagined." Something to which I whole-heartedly concurred. Another fellow mourner facetiously remarked, "The way he courted the ladies, I always figured Scatucci might get shot by some jealous husband. But sure as hell never pictured anything like this."

There were several speeches made, most quite short, in contrast to the old joke about lawyers rambling on and on as if they got paid by the word. Perhaps it was for lack of preparation in light of the sudden death and quick cremation. "Helluva lawyer, helluva guy. Gonna be missed," one simply said, a summary of what all assembled were feeling.

Among the numbers of friends and colleagues were two family members: his daughter and his sister. The funeral was my first-time meeting Vinnie's sister. I found her to be a delightful woman, though lacking the charisma and outgoing personality of her brother. Plain in appearance, soft-spoken and demure. If you were casting a mild-mannered, prim, middle-aged Midwestern woman for a movie, she would be it. "Vinnie," she explained, "was the pride of our family. He was clearly the favorite. Our dad thought the sun rose and set in him. I did too, I guess. My brother and I were quite close growing up. When he moved here to California, we sorta drifted apart but I have always been so proud of him. I cannot believe he is gone. It is simply beyond my ability to grasp the circumstances of his death. I just have no words."

His daughter, whom I'd only met a few times before, was just as poised and beautiful as Vinnie always described her. Speaking with Gina was a sorrow-filled experience, my heart breaking even as I did my best to console. "Your dad was a great guy," I told her honestly. "And a damn good lawyer, too. He had the convincing charm of a politician. Judges liked him. Juries liked him. And he was a fun friend. I really enjoyed his company." And now he was gone.

His ashes had been placed in an urn that Gina held tightly

in her lap. At some point, she stood up and walked to the edge of the rooftop, carrying the urn. "If you all might rise," she addressed the collection of mourners. "I will now be scattering my father's ashes in accordance with the way he once told me. At the time I believed he was only joking, but who am I to second-guess how he wanted this to go?"

Leaning out over the edge of the roofline, she emptied the contents of the urn over the side, a puff of gray ash carried by the night breeze, rising in the air like a cloud and drifting off toward the marina below. "I'm pretty sure this is illegal – casting human remains off a city rooftop," she announced. "Which is why I know this is exactly what he wanted." A gentle chuckle rose among the group, followed by spontaneous applause.

A couple months have now passed since Scatucci's funeral. Sadly, I've come to accept the fact that my friend killed himself and his law clerk over money. I thought I knew Vinnie better than that, but how well do we ever truly know anyone?

## CHAPTER FORTY

The phone rang. Samantha looked at the number displayed on her cell phone. A weird number. One she'd never seen before. She ignored the call. Minutes later, it rang again. Same weird number. And then a third time. "Who the hell is this?" she shouted, annoyed, finally answering the call.

"Sam, don't hang up," she heard the caller say, the voice sounding muffled, but familiar. "It's me, Gavin."

"Oh my God! Oh my God! Oh my God! Gavin? Is that really you?"

"Yea, Sam, it's me."

"Oh my God! Thank you, Lord! Where are you? We all thought you were dead."

"I can't tell you where I am. Just wanna let you know I'm okay."

"Gavin! Talk to me. I need to know what's going on. My entire life has been discombobulated since you went missing. I never thought I'd ever hear your voice again. And now …"

"Connie tried to kill me," he softly interrupted, his voice sounding remarkably calm and relaxed.

"Yes, we know. We thought she *did* have you killed. Oh Gavin, I've been so worried, so upset. What happened?"

"The Lord was not ready to call me home yet," Gavin told her. "God intervened. I feel so blessed. The guy Connie sent to murder me had a change of heart. Can you imagine that? A hired killer sent to do a job and he changes his mind. He could'a killed me. Connie could'a gotten away with it. But the Lord had other plans. Jesus saved me."

"How? What happened?" She was incredulous.

He related the story of how he had been out enjoying a perfect day of fishing, how his engines had failed, then another boat approached, and a man said he'd been sent to kill him. "But instead of murdering me, the killer just got back into his boat and then pulled away. Left me stranded fifty miles from land on *Bite Me* with a stalled engine. He took my cell phone and the boat's radio, tossed them overboard. Maybe he just figgered I would die out there on my own without him having to do it himself. Thank the Lord, I had a deflated Zodiac and outboard stored in an aft lazarette. Better to have and not need, than to need and not have I always say. I pumped up the dinghy, left the fishing boat behind, and headed back in the direction of Oahu. Unfortunately, the outboard ran outa gas after about an hour. I started rowing but was still way too far from land. No way I could'a rowed that far to shore."

"Holy crap, Gavin! What did you do?"

"It was pretty scary having that guy try to kill me, but floating around in that dinghy all by myself miles from land became even more scary. Believe me, there is nothing more desert-like than being stranded in the hot sun on the ocean with nowhere to go for shade or drinking water. I bobbed around for hours getting fried in the sun and practically dying of thirst. And then it happened."

"What happened? What Gavin?" Samantha implored.

"I don't know what I did to deserve being saved again, but

Jesus stepped in once more. I spotted a flash out on the far horizon. Just a glimmer at first. Pretty soon I realized it was a sailboat, way out there. I could barely make out the mast and sail sticking up, barely visible. Praise God! I stood up in the dinghy and fired off a flare that was in the inflatable's side pocket. The sailboat skipper saw it and headed toward me. He asked what in God's name I was doing that far out in a tiny rubber boat. I played dumb, told him I wasn't paying proper attention, and the currents just swept me out to sea. When we got back to his marina at Kaneohe, I thanked him and promised I'd be more careful in the future."

"Oh Gav, what a miracle," Sammie said, her voice filled with emotion.

"For sure, it was," Gavin agreed. "But I worried if the killer discovered I was still alive he might wanna come back and finish the job. So, ever since then, I've just been hiding out. I had enough money on me to ride the bus over to Hawaii Kai. A fishing buddy of mine lives there, has a boat in that little marina. He let me crash there on the boat. Said I was welcome to stay as long as I needed. Probably never dreamed I'd stay so long, but I wasn't sure what to do. I've been too afraid to show myself. I mean, who knows? Every day I wonder if that killer might show up wanting to finish the job. And Connie? How could she have betrayed me like that? How could I have been so foolish as to think she'd found the Lord and had left her sinful past behind? I had forgiven the debauchery of her past. I know the things she did, the things she made men do. So many men. But sending some guy to murder me, her own husband! Forgive me Lord, everybody has their limitations ... and this guy's the limit! I've gone from angry, to confused, to fear and back again. I'm still not sure what to do. But it's been so long. I can't just remain in hiding forever."

"Gavin, Connie is dead."

"What? How?" Gavin was truly befuddled.

"She was arrested on murder charges. Accused of murdering, or conspiring to murder, you."

"Well, good. She *did* try to kill me," Gavin agreed.

"While she was incarcerated, someone murdered *her*. How's that for Divine justice?"

"God does not work like that, Samantha. This is terrible news."

"Oh, sweet Gavin. I simply cannot believe you have been hiding out like some terrified hunted animal all this time. That you survived. Maybe there really is a God. There's no need to hide any longer. You should go home," Sammie suggested. "Absolutely. Tell the police what happened to you. I'll fly out and stay with you for a while."

# CHAPTER FORTY-ONE

In the courtroom, speaking from her elevated seat on the bench, swishing aside the bulky sleeves of her loose-fitting black robe as she leaned forward on her elbows, the Honorable Amy G. Dala spelled it all out for Rojas Raton.

"Given its location on the border of Mexico," the judge began, "California is considered a hotbed for drug trafficking, both into the state from Mexico and also to neighboring states. Importing drugs from another country is considered a very serious crime in California. A person commits the crime of drug trafficking when manufacturing, distributing, dispensing, or possessing with the intent to manufacture, distribute, or dispense any amount of a prohibited narcotic.

"The state of California and the federal government have adopted a classification method, a schedule if you will, for illegal substances that is based on how potentially dangerous they can be. Schedule Two includes drugs considered to be the most dangerous. This is based mainly on their high risk of addiction with no practical medical use. Cocaine is a Schedule Two drug under Section 11055 (b)(6)."

Stopping for several moments, her eyes looking down, lips silently moving as she read to herself from some papers in front of her, the judge then continued.

"In California, the sale or transportation of drugs under Health and Safety Code Section 11352 is a felony. The standard penalties for these types of code violations could include prison time of three to nine years.

"Federal charges for drug trafficking, however, are far more serious than state charges. A person arrested by the FBI, DEA, or other federal agency, as we have here, for transporting drugs across a state or national border will face Federal charges, and conviction in Federal Court for transporting five kilograms or more of cocaine can result in a *minimum* of ten years in prison. The maximum and minimum penalties are generally contained in 21 U.S.C. Section 841. If a large quantity of drug was being trafficked, life imprisonment may also be an option.

"Of course, a complaint is only a charge and is not evidence of guilt.  Charges are only allegations, and the defendant is presumed innocent unless and until proven guilty beyond a reasonable doubt." A date was then set for trial to commence.

Investigated by the Drug Enforcement Administration, the FBI, IRS-Criminal Investigation, as well as local and state police departments, searches were made of Raton's San Diego, California residence and found $111,995 hidden inside a pillow openly displayed on a bedroom chair that during trial he conceded was illicit drug proceeds. They also found marijuana, a drug ledger, pay/owe sheets showing what people paid and owed him for drugs, and a loaded XD 9mm semi-automatic handgun. Over the course of only a few years, Raton managed to obtain substantial sums of money from his involvement in the drug-trafficking conspiracy which he converted to other forms of property, such as real estate, including an apartment located in Naples, Italy to which his name appeared on title, in an effort to conceal the illicit nature of the drug proceeds.

The trial of Ricardo Salvadore Rojas, more commonly known as Rojas Raton, was prosecuted by Assistant U.S. Attorney Ian M. Krulle and received national news coverage. Rojas was found to be a primary organizer in a drug-trafficking organization that distributed substantial amounts of cocaine from Mexico and throughout California, Arizona, and Nevada. In the end, Rojas ultimately admitted that he was the mastermind and personally responsible for the distribution of well in excess of 450 kilograms of cocaine during his involvement with the larger conspiracy. At one point, he was distributing approximately 10 to 20 kilograms of cocaine each week, much of it in liquid form hidden in wine bottles.

Rose Emsch, the widow of the now deceased Eddy Emsch, and co-owner of the winery involved in the drug trafficking operation, was granted full immunity from prosecution in exchange for her testimony against the accused kingpin, Rojas Raton. Her key testimony was damning. Before his death, before she had left the winery for safer quarters, her husband confessed to her, in specific detail, his involvement with Raton. In her testimony – overcoming multiple hearsay objections – Rose divulged all he had told her, including that her husband was not merely working under the aegis of Rojas Raton but that he had been forcefully compelled, against his will, to cooperate with Raton.

Ricardo Salvadore Rojas, a Columbian national residing in the United States at San Diego, California was sentenced in federal court for his role in a conspiracy that distributed more than 2,600 kilograms of cocaine throughout the state of California and other states. He was the kingpin and final defendant among thirteen defendants found guilty and to be sentenced in this case, ten being Mexican nationals, two others being U.S. citizens. Rojas received twelve years in federal prison without parole. The court also ordered him to forfeit to the government $12,150,000, which represents the proceeds of his illegal drug trafficking.

Rojas was never charged with the crime of murder. No evidence was ever discovered connecting him to the murder of Eddy Emsch, or anyone else for that matter. Rose Emsch, however, knew who had murdered her husband. She knew, with absolute certainty, that it was the late Connie Cantu-Gambil, though no one could seem to figure out how she might have pulled it off. Still, with Raton in prison and Cantu-Gambil dead, it allowed Rose grim solace, a perfect example of justice being best served cold.

## CHAPTER FORTY-TWO

Prison is an ugly word. A despicable place filled with mostly despicable inmates and, some would argue, an inhumane concept. Within its walls are multitudes of people who broke a serious rule of society, some violent, some not. There are also, unfortunately, some innocent people in prisons throughout the nation. More than two million Americans are in prison. In a country of 330 million, that makes for the highest incarceration rate in the world.

The reason for prisons is to keep society safe and exercising the need to be tough on crime but, in reality, prison as a vehicle may have little to do with safety or deterrence of crime. It is far more about societal vengeance than it is about redemption, but it's what we do. We send "bad guys" to prison.

Rojas Raton was, and remains, a very bad guy. Many might say a monster. To keep such a man behind bars, removed from the rest of society, would almost certainly be considered a justified necessity. But for how long? Twelve years in federal prison may easily feel like a lifetime to an inmate, while seeming overly brief to victims left in the wake of a crime.

Be that as it may, even the most hardened criminals have difficulty adjusting to a life deprived of freedom, economic stability, pursuit of health and happiness, and possibly even basic medical treatments that are outside the limited capabilities of the institution. A prisoner's emotional state while incarcerated often fluctuates between the five stages of incarceration – denial, anger, bargaining, depression, acceptance – derived from the traditional stages of grief outlined by American Swiss psychiatrist, Elisabeth Kubler-Ross. Like everyone, prisoners are processing and responding to what is happening in their lives. These stages are not necessarily linear since prisoners can flow in and out of them. But often a prisoner's behavior can be explained by where they are within these stages.

Rojas Raton had not yet reached the stage of acceptance. Doubtful he ever would. He was pissed off that he had ever hired that damn dago lawyer Scatucci. Who the hell told him Scatucci was the best defense attorney anyway? That was some very bad advice. That dumb-fucking lawyer may have somehow kept that Bambini broad out of prison, but totally failed when it came to representing a far greater figure like him – the infamous Rojas Raton.

What a fucking pussy, too. So, Raton leaned on Scatucci a little to make a point but he sure as hell never figured his lawyer would go and off himself. Put a bullet in his own head. What the fuck? Weren't those dago wops supposed to be tougher than that? He had seen The Godfather movies. What the hell was this world coming to? You just can't count on anything anymore. Screw him, good riddance.

All his hidden cash was now gone. Scatucci fucked him out of a quarter million bucks. His goddamn Jew law clerk pissed it all away, and Scatucci let it happen. Both of them worthless dumb fucks. The cops found all the other hidden money. Even the cash he had hidden in a pillow at his house was confiscated. Without being able to get his hands on any other funds, they tried to saddle him with some overworked court ordered defense attorney assigned to his case. No way! Raton found himself a different high-priced attorney, this one willing to take the case without any damned retainer, happy to take it just because it was a really big case. Highly publicized. One that could make the lawyer famous for defending. Turned out the only thing that fame-hungry lawyer got famous for is losing the biggest drug case in a decade because, in the end, Raton got convicted anyway. Even without testimony from that faggot Eddy Emsch, there was enough evidence produced to convict Rojas on all the drug charges. Emsch's wife's testimony seemed to seal that deal. Raton was toast.

But to Raton it wasn't over. Sooner or later, he would get released. One way or another. And there were still scores to be settled. Señora Emsch testified about things she may yet live to regret. And he was still pissed about the whole Scatucci fiasco.

To pass time, inmates would sometimes play a game called who did the most brutal and coolest crime. On one such occasion Raton claimed to have murdered a man by slicing off his genitals, dressing the victim in drag, cutting out his tongue, and hanging him from a rafter until he bled to death. "Gave him what the Feds call a Columbian necktie. And I made it all happen while stuck here behind these bars," he bragged. A number of fellow inmates told their own tales, trying to top that one. "Ah," Rojas added, a sardonic smile revealing a single gold tooth that stood out amongst the rest of his pearly whites, "but then I took that poor fucker's severed cock and balls, his whole goddam package, and stuffed it down the throat of his girlfriend. Made her choke on it till she suffocated and died."

## CHAPTER FORTY-THREE

# BEN HARDING

We recently closed probate on Vincent Scatucci's estate. Though I've never done much probate work in my legal career, Vinnie's daughter asked me to be the probate attorney. Much like when Samantha asked the same of me when her husband died, how could I refuse?

Over the course of nearly a year, the beach condo was sold off, as were the Ferrari, the BMW, and all the other worldly goods that made up Vinnie's high-roller universe. Expensive designer suits, ties, and shoes – the clothes of a dead man – had no enduring value and were mostly donated to charity.

I was contacted by no fewer than four different women, ages twenty-four to fifty-four, all claiming to be Scatucci's fiancé and asking if they might be entitled to a part of his estate. All claims of betrothal were totally bogus, of course. Besides, absent a specific devise in a will, fiancés are not considered beneficiaries of an estate. Only spouses. And, if there is one thing of which I am certain, it is that Vinnie never intended to marry again. He had made that clear on numerous occasions. "Once was more than enough," he often said. "For me, getting divorced was like getting fired from a job I'd hated for years."

The sole heir to Vinnie's estate was his daughter, Gina Scatucci. I suggested she move in and take over the Marina del Rey condo, but she declined. "Too many memories," she said. "I kinda grew up there. It would always feel like my dad's place, never my own. Besides, I have no interest in living at the beach. Unlike my dad, who absolutely hated cold weather and snow, I'm a mountain gal. He moved to California to escape cold weather and I'd prefer to escape Los Angeles and be where it's cold." The cash from the sale was more than enough for her to buy a cabin up at Big Bear, and that is precisely what she did.

Also, she had no interest in her father's diplomas, bar awards, news clippings, or other memorabilia. I asked her why and she just shrugged. Perhaps the hurt was just too new? Maybe it was too soon for her to deal with such personal items, but I just could not bring myself to throw it all in the trash. I boxed up the more important items and am storing them in my garage. I suspect she may want these things one day and I will be happy to deliver them to her.

It felt a bit creepy wandering about in my friend's condo, rummaging through his things. Like an interloper, uninvited, but someone had to do it. I came across hundreds of photographs as I sorted. Boxes of them. Snapshots of Scatucci as a teenager with high school pals, all looking so young and happy. Several of Vinnie wearing a school baseball uniform, sometimes swinging a bat, or catching a ball in mid-air. Photos in his Detroit police uniform too. Wedding pictures of him with his former wife. Baby photos, Vinnie holding his infant daughter. I was trespassing into his early former life. The Vinnie I never knew. Also, more recent stuff. Photos taken at parties and other social functions showing Vinnie with celebrities and local politicians. Lots and lots of photos of him with beautiful women, many quite risqué. It hit me that all of these, the ones from a distant past as well as the more recent, were a visual history of this man's life, documentation of his personal evolution. A life that I'm certain he never would have intentionally choreographed to have had such a brutal ending. A life to which I merely shared one very tiny fraction of. I feel lucky to have called him a friend and hope he may have felt the same.

As the probate process was winding down, a bank downtown contacted me as the estate's attorney about a safe deposit box they had in Vincent's name. I drove into the city myself to retrieve the contents of the box. I didn't have the key, so they had to drill the small private safe door open in order to get to the individual box contained therein. I was then shown into a private room where I opened the box. I don't know if what I found there is more disturbing or relieving, but the answers to all my questions about Vinnie's death were inside that little tin box, in an unmailed handwritten letter addressed to me.

*Ben old buddy,*

*This will likely be the very last letter I will ever write in my life and if you are reading this you know what I've done. I just want to explain myself. Explain it to you, paesan, because you're the only one I can trust with this information.*

*Of course, you know Rivlen, my law clerk. And I know you are aware that he is an ex-con, a convicted felon. He had a gambling habit that kept getting him into trouble. He's also a former client. We got to know each other when I was representing him in a criminal matter. I discovered that he was a really bright guy. A self-taught student of the law. In prison he had plenty of time to study from law books he found there.*

*He could have been a damn good lawyer, were it not for his felony conviction keeping him from becoming a member of the bar. When he got released, I gave him a job when nobody else would, and helped him hone his legal research skills. Turned out, he is great at that humdrum shit, a better researcher than I ever will be. He's worked for me for nearly a decade without a hitch. Until now.*

*He fucked up big time. I mean really BIG TIME! Embezzled a quarter million dollars of client money, then went off on a gambling spree and pissed it all away. I thought his out-of-control gambling days were over. Sadly, I was wrong. Know whose money it was that he stole? Rojas Raton. Drug cartel money. So, I'm sure you will agree that when I say he fucked up big time, I'm not exaggerating. When I told Raton what happened, he completely blew up. That was his nest-egg emergency fund that he had stashed away to be used at times like he was currently finding himself in. He called Rivlen a dead man.*

*The money Randy gambled away was my retainer fee. So, technically Rivlen stole the money from me, not Raton. But Raton did not see it that way. He took it as a personal affront and decided Rivlen could not be allowed to get away with such a diss. I told Raton the retainer no longer mattered, that I would represent him pro bono, for free. But that did not calm his ass down. In fact, it only seemed to anger him more. He told me that Rivlen had to die, and since it was ultimately my fault that Rivlen got his hands on the money, he demanded that I be the one to do the deed. Of course, I refused.*

*That's when Raton said if I refused, he'd put a hit on me. I'm a former cop and don't take well to threats, so told Raton to go screw himself. Ben, that turned out to be a big mistake.*

*A few days ago Raton sent over one of his thugs who*

related a new message – Raton no longer wanted to kill me…
he was going to kill my daughter Gina instead!

I contacted Raton and pleaded with him to leave Gina
alone. I told him that I would not only get him the money and
represent him for free, but I'd also stay on retainer as long as
he needed me, both now and in the future. I offered to be his
consigliere. But, by this time, Raton no longer wanted me as his
lawyer or the money … he wanted to set an example – someone
had to die!

Ben, I begged this fucking asshole. I begged for my
daughter's life. In the end, he gave me one grizzly option. He
said if I killed Rivlen myself, then he would spare Gina – but
only if I do it in a way that does not implicate Raton in any
way. Ben, I want you to know, I have no choice in this. I
must protect my daughter. I've even convinced myself that my
scumbag law clerk _deserves_ to die. But if I'm a killer, then I
guess I deserve to die too.

Ben, I hope I can trust you on this. What I want is for you
to someday let Gina know the truth about why I did what I
did. BUT you can only tell her years from now; after Raton
has died of old age or whatever it is that finally claims him.
Even if he is locked up in a prison cell, as long as he is alive he
still wields power. Otherwise, if word gets out and the police
tie him to this in any way, I fear he will have Gina killed. I'm
well-versed in his case and more than likely the guy will be
spending considerable time behind bars. But this is the type of
dude who will carry a grudge forever. Sooner or later, he will
be out and would not hesitate to harm her. Please Ben, as my
friend, honor my wishes on this.

Ciao paesan,
Vinnie

I closed out Vinnie's deposit box account and opened one of my own, locking his letter in the very same bank vault … where it will remain until the time is right.

## CHAPTER FORTY-FOUR

t was a warm evening, the sun setting behind Santa Catalina Island, sea gulls pinwheeling in the darkening sky. Samantha took a sip from her wine glass, then turned her face toward Ben, a strange half smile and languorous look in her eyes. She could see the glow of the sunset reflected in his sunglasses. It had taken years, since high school in fact, but she had at last reached a conclusion about this man and his role in her life.

Offering a girlish smile, seemingly out of the blue she said, "The answer is a definite yes and no."

"Say what?" Ben asked, confused. "Yes and no about what?"

"The night you picked me up at LAX. When I returned from visiting Gavin in Hawaii. I was so relieved because he was back on his boat, alive and well. Gavin took such total comfort in the knowledge that everything that had happened to him was God's will, part of God's plan. I found myself wishing I could have such faith in anything or anyone. Then, when I saw your face at the terminal, it occurred to me that, in all the world, you are the one single person in whom I have the most faith. You're the only one I can trust. I mean, truly trust. No matter what happens, I know I can always rely on you."

"Oh, thank you, sweetie. Please don't ever doubt it. You

are the most important person in the world to me. And I'm so relieved it all turned out well for Gavin. Right from the get-go, you knew Gavin was being hoodwinked by Cantu. You were right on the money with that one, I'd say."

"Well, even a blind squirrel is correct twice a day," she replied.

He loved this woman and every malapropism she ever uttered. "Yes," he said, looking at her with an amused smile, "that is true."

She reached past Ben to retrieve the bottle of wine that was sitting on the rail of the outside deck where they were seated. Looking at the label, Paniolo Rose Winery. "I wonder whatever happened to that nice woman at the winery," Samantha said. "I feel so sorry for her. All she went through."

"We should drive out there," Ben replied. "Pay her a visit. See if there's anything we can do for her. Replenish our supply of her excellent vino, too."

"Oh yes, let's do that, Ben. Let's do that soon, okay?"

"Sure thing. A fun day in the country. Sounds good to me."

"Thank you." She moved closer, resting her head on his shoulder.

"So, those answers you mentioned?"

She sat upright once more, looking at him face to face. "Sooo, the answer to the first question is yes. Yes, I will move in with you. There is nowhere I would rather be than right here with you, in this fine old house, overlooking the ocean."

Ben pulled her close and they kissed. Her face touching his. At age forty-nine, she was every bit as attractive as when they'd met in high school. He admired every incipient wrinkle in her face, loved every pore on her nose. They sat close, in a warm embrace as the first cool wisp of evening breeze arrived.

"You said there were two answers?" he asked at last.

"You also asked if I would marry you. My answer is no. At

least not right now. I love you, Ben. But I've been married before. You've been married before. It's over-rated, don't you think? Let's just be together because we love each other. Not for any other reason."

Ben reached for the bottle, filling each of their glasses. Raising his glass, he toasted: "Sometimes life actually exceeds your dreams. To us. Long may we love." They clinked glasses.

"To us," Samantha repeated. "Wherever we are."

## THE END

ABOUT THE AUTHOR

MICHAEL E. PETRIE is a surfer, sailor, musician, and former rodeo cowboy turned attorney and award-winning writer whose work has appeared in numerous publications. He lives with his wife, children, dogs, and horse in California.

Videos of his ocean-crossing sailing experiences and samples of his music can be found on YouTube at Michael E Petrie

www.ingramcontent.com/pod-product-compliance
Lightning Source LLC
Chambersburg PA
CBHW050318110726
47899CB00007B/2289